# Stramullion

**a Scottish-based feminist publishing collective**

# Moll Cutpurse

Published by Stramullion Co-operative Ltd.
43 Candlemaker Row, Edinburgh EH1 2QB.
Project co-ordinator Joy Pitman, assisted by Moira Turnbull and members of
    Stramullion.
Book design by Joy Pitman and Susie Innes.
Cover design, illustrations and calligraphy Susie Innes.
Cover illustration from title page of *The Roaring Girl* by permission of the
    British Library.
Many of the illustrations are based on contemporary herbals.


Typeset in 11/13 Bembo by E.U.S.P.B., 1 Buccleuch Place,
    Edinburgh EH8 9LW.


Printed by Redwood Burn Ltd., Yeoman Way, Trowbridge,
    Wiltshire BA14 0QL.


Distributed by Scottish and Northern Book Distribution Co-operative Ltd.
    48a Hamilton Place, Edinburgh EH3 5AY
    and 18 Granby Row, Manchester M1 3PE.

ISBN 0 907343 03 1

# THE AUTHOR

ELLEN GALFORD wrote this, her first novel, while a
member of the women's writers group which
produced the poetry anthology *Hens in the Hay* —
Stramullion's first publication. She has worked in
publishing, television, and for the Edinburgh Film
Festival. She is now living in London and writing her
second novel.

For Ellen Smyth and the East Preston Street comrades.

# Moll Cutpurse
## Her True History

Ellen Galford

MOLL CUTPURSE was never one for keeping secrets. Whoever first named her the Roaring Girl was no liar. She had a voice like a bellowing ox and a laugh like a lovesick lion — and when she strutted through the streets the crowds parted and stood goggling.

The little coneys and bumpkins, up from muddy villages for a once-in-a-lifetime look at London, stared with their mouths gaping, puzzling over this monster that was halfway between man and woman. They'd shake their heads, and add the sight to the list of marvels they'd tell the friends back home, too bedazzled to feel the dextrous passage of a stranger's fingers through an unguarded purse.

Even the Londoners, who'd sooner be clapped in the pillory than be caught looking surprised, would pause to study her appearance and hear her latest pronunciamentos. She was a legend before she was five-and-twenty. They even made a comedy about her, and she went to see it at the playhouse in Golding Lane, sitting up on the stage and laughing so loud they had to hush her, or no one would have heard the players.

Moll loved an audience; she'd have been a player herself if they'd have let her. Half the stories spread about her were lies and fables, the others only a pale, watery version of the truth. Moll never minded — she loved to be at the centre of it all, and if there weren't enough tales with her name in them abroad in Paul's Churchyard and Cheapside, she'd grow restless and start up a few new rumours herself.

But there was one secret she did keep, and that was the secret of our life together. Being close-mouthed and discreet about anything was harder than all Hercules' labours for Moll, yet she did this, as she did so many things, to please me.

Now, so many years later, I feel the time has come to yield up that secret. Or all that will be left to keep alive Moll's memory will be the fabrications of *men*. The famous play about her was writ when Moll was young enough and strong enough to break the heads of the playwrights if it displeased her, and those who wrote it were her old boozing-companions in any case. But lately, some dull scribbler who never knew her has taken it upon himself to tell her story. Some of the tales he tells are true enough, but he has passed them off as Moll's own diary and that is a foul lie. Moll never wrote a diary in her life. And all the way through his text, this catchpenny scribe seems to leer and laugh at her, with his tongue in his cheek, as if my Moll were a curiosity like the two-headed calf or the anthropophagi.

So it falls to me, because I knew her best and loved her most, to tell Roaring Moll's true story, and my own with it.

IF MY father had had a son I would never have learned to read and write. He was a herbalist by trade, a dabbler in alchemy and magic. Nothing on the grand scale of Dr Dee or Simon Forman, but well thought of in the parish of St Bride's. He had more wild ideas than good sense, more mess to clear up than money coming in, so he needed someone who would help in his work and ask no pay. Even apprentices, though unwaged, require a certain amount of expenditure, although you wouldn't think it if you saw the emaciated children who toil in my fat neighbour's workshop. Sons would have been the ideal solution, my father thought, and he kept hoping that my mother would give him one. She thought so too, and died trying. So my father was left with me as his only hope, and consoled himself with my speed at learning to read and cipher. He was a cheerful, comfortable man, forgetful of his own surroundings, interested mainly in his studies. So I grew up knowing less about the housewifely arts than I did about the black ones.

We made our living, such as it was, on the spells and potions needed by the neighbourhood. Over the years I had learned enough about herbs and simples to take care of most of our trade myself, leaving my father free to get on with his great experiments, or lose himself in the works of Agrippa and Paracelsus. The good-wives of the district, who brought us eggs or pies in exchange for backache powders and soothing syrups, worried about me. "If your dear mother was still alive, you'd be a wife by now. This is no life for a fine girl like you."

"No dowry," I'd reply with downcast eyes. That shut them up; they went away clucking sympathetically. But the truth was, I'd learned all I wanted about married life from the women who came to our shop:

"Can you give me something to make my husband lust after me?"

"Can you give me something to make my husband leave me alone?"

"Can you give me something to ease a long labour?"

"Can you give me something to make my baby sleep at night?"

13

"Can you give me something to keep my strength up?"

These requests, and others like them, provided a large part of our trade, and we dosed the neighbourhood through its seasons of chills and fevers. But we had other, stranger custom: hooded figures, tapping on the shutters late at night, murmuring of fast-acting poisons, or, sometimes, whispering of powders that would be slow but deadly, allowing the victim to repent in agony, revealing all secrets, while white-hot snakes slid through his vitals. These last demands were never met, no matter what sums we were offered—but I do confess that once or twice, when we were truly on the verge of starvation, we'd cross ourselves and hand over a paper filled with something quick, efficient and relatively painless. Still, it may be a word in our favour that whatever food we bought with such earnings always stuck in our throats and tasted of ashes.

Then one day, when my father was muttering to himself over Ficino's Book of Life, and I was mixing a stock of spring tonics, someone banged open the door and pounded into the shop.

"Damn you," I muttered into my powders, vexed at the interruption. I wanted to finish my work and go for a walk in the sunshine. Then I looked up to meet the eyes of the strangest woman I'd ever seen.

"Turn me into a man," was all she said.

$S$HE was of middling height, stout and thickset, with short-cropped yellow hair that looked as if it had been struck off in desperation with a blunted knife. She was dressed in a rough jerkin and breeches, and carried a tobacco pipe. If I hadn't heard her speak I might have taken her for a boy. The look in her eyes was at once fierce and frightened, and for a moment I thought she might be some mad moonstruck runaway from the Bedlam. I stood and stared.

"I don't care what it costs. I've plenty of money."

There is one golden rule in our business: never say that any request, no matter how far-fetched, is impossible to fulfil. If one mixture doesn't work, charge them double and try another. Sooner or later either their purse or their patience will give out. But this was no easy matter of camomile for a woman's monthly pains, or a love-philtre to blind a haughty virgin to her suitor's pimples. So I brought her into the back of the shop, to find my father peering out eagerly from his mountain of books. He might have been a dreamer, but he wasn't deaf, and his ears always pricked up at the sound of something interesting.

"A very challenging case, my dear," he pronounced, stroking his beard. "The task you set us isn't an easy one, although there are precedents among the ancients for all manner of metamorphoses. To wit, Tiresias, who turned from man to woman and back again, or the hapless Lucius who found himself transformed into an ass. And, of course, the sorceress Circe altered men into swine."

"Not a great alteration, that," I observed. Our visitor looked offended.

"I don't want to be an ass or a pig," she cried, "or find myself changed over and back again like your Ti-re-whatever. But I'm sure I'm not meant to be a woman."

"Well, then," said my father, "you must sit down and take some of our excellent cowslip wine — courtesy of the house, of course — and tell us about yourself. Then my daughter and I will consider the best way to help you."

This, as I remember it, is the tale she told us.

MY name's Moll Frith. They christened me Mary, but it never sat right. You might know my father — he's the shoemaker in Aldersgate Street — but he won't thank you if you tell him you've seen me. He says I'll be the death of him, and I haven't been home for six months. I live where I can; right now I lodge with old Mother Bunch at her alehouse in Chick Lane. She stinks of beer and piss, and my room's a foul closet, but she doesn't ask any questions. There's no rent to pay as long as I help shovel out the drunkards last thing at night, and throw down some fresh straw on the floor every morning.

I think I'm eighteen. My mother told me I was walking and talking well before the Spaniards sent their Armada. My father says if he knew then what he knows now, he would have shot me off to the King of Spain in a cannon.

My mother broke her heart and a hundred switches trying to teach me to spin and sew. She'd set me to stitch a seam or a row of buttons, turning to her own work, and five minutes later find me missing. I'd be playing at Cudgels or Turks and Christians with the boys in our lane. I hated women's work — the snipping, the knitting, worst of all the sitting still — and my efforts were so poor that you might have thought I'd sewn my samplers with my feet, like the poor armless girl at Bartholomew Fair. I wouldn't do it, and I couldn't do it, and my mother despaired. I wanted to run about the docks and grow up to be a water-man, or sail with Sir Francis Drake, conquering the world in the Queen's service. What did I want with sweeping and sewing? And as for cookery, what need for it in London, with good, cheap ordinaries in every street, and the pie-woman with her stinking-meat pies?

But none of these arguments impressed my mother. And when I broke the nose of an apprentice in my father's shop, for calling me a mewling *girl*, my parents decided it was beyond their powers to change me.

"The only way you'll get her off your hands is to put her into service," my uncle — who was their counsellor in all things — advised them. "That's what she needs. A spell in a well-run household under a major-domo with a short temper for fools and laggards. Twelve months and you won't recognise her."

"Who ever would have her?" asked my father.

"Leave it to me," said my aunt. She knew a woman whose husband's sister was pastry cook in a great house — "Where her word is law because they're afraid to lose her. The Duchess of Kent herself praised her sugar-work swans and said she'd have the woman away from her master."

So I was put to be a servant in a great lord's

household. My aunt, who brought me there, didn't exactly lie about me, just said I was a strong, healthy girl, and left the servants' hall to discover the rest at its peril.

There were two dozen servants belonging to the house, and many more that number at my lord's estates in the country. I never found out precisely what everyone did: some worked in the laundry, some in the kitchen, some looked after the upstairs rooms. The family had their personal attendants — maids and valets and the children's nurses — but these were a race apart, for they had their own hall and we hardly ever saw them.

The majordomo took one look at me and decided I wouldn't do for the upper chambers, so I was put to work in the kitchen, scrubbing pots and turning the spit. It could have been worse: it was a cold winter when I came and the heat of the kitchen was a welcome relief, in the beginning. I liked my food, and more of it came my way than was really intended. Not only did I grow expert at filching morsels off the serving platters, but all the kitchen servants enjoyed the unofficial perquisite of extra rations: the cook turned a blind eye and juggled the household accounts. But I hated washing pots — the household dirtied more basins and tureens and chafing dishes at one meal than my mother used in a year. I wasn't very good at it, either. The cook, inspecting my work, would fall into a screaming fury, and no matter how many kicks and cuffs she gave me, I could never quite manage to scour away the grease and the burnt bits.

I didn't mind turning the spit, though. They told me it was usually a boy's job, which pleased me greatly. It was heavy work, but left me time to daydream. Some days I never stopped, cranking away at sides of beef, haunches of venison, rows of skewered quail and partridge for breakfast, dinner, nuncheons, supper and reresupper. The house was always full of guests, and my lord delighted in giving feasts for fifty or a hundred at one time. Whenever the majordomo appeared with a list of instructions as long as his arm, the cook and the pastry-cook would roll their eyes heavenwards, curse, grumble about the miracle of the loaves and fishes, and then leap into action, shouting orders to the rest of us. They wheeled about the kitchen like whirlwinds, almost too fast for the eye to see, producing sauces, puddings, great sculpted cakes of marchpane and spun sugar, gleaming jellies, rivers of fish, herds of roasted beeves, mountains of suckets that glittered like the jewels on my lady's gowns.

Someontimes, by the time I'd finished keeling the pots from an evening's feast, it was time to start roasting the meat for the family's breakfast. Mornings like those I cursed my lot and cried some secret tears in the chimney corner, wanting to go home, wishing I'd never been sent here. The cook would be in a foul temper all day long, and the rest of us would snap and snarl at each other like our master's spaniels, quarrelling over the scraps from his table.

But there was one consolation, in the lovely shape of Meg the kitchenmaid. From where I stood at the spit I could see her moving about her work, sharpening knives, grinding spices, cutting up fruit. She always seemed happy, never snuffling and sullen as I was, singing little songs to herself as she bent over her mortar or chopping board. She was a little older than I was, and had been in service a year longer. The steam of the kitchen may have reddened her hands and coarsened her skin, but to me she was fairer than any of the ladies who came to dine in the great hall.

She smiled at me, as she smiled at everyone, but rarely spoke. I racked my brains trying to think of things to say to her, to let her know I was brave and clever and strong, without making her think I was vainglorious as well. Sometimes the cook would put her to basting the roasting meat with wine and spices, and I'd stand there, turning the spit, quivering with delight at having her so close by.

The servants all slept on straw pallets in a warren of little rooms behind the buttery, except for the majordomo and the cooks, who had proper bedchambers. I'd been sleeping beside the old still-room maid, whose rattling snores penetrated into my dreams, where they assumed the shape of howling wolves and evil spirits. But one day, after I'd been several months in the household, Meg stopped by the basin where I stood scrubbing pots, and asked if I'd mind becoming her bedfellow. The two laundrymaids who'd shared her closet had been caught pilfering my lady's pillowslips to sell to a pedlar, and they'd been turned out of the house in disgrace. We'd all heard the news; the servants' hall had talked of nothing else for days. Meg had been on her own for three nights, but much as she hated to confess it, she had a mortal fear of the dark, and hadn't slept a wink in all that time. I was in ecstasy.

Moving my goods presented no problem. I kept all my possessions in a little wooden box: my night-smock, a spare shift, a cloak, two pairs of knitted hose that were my mother's parting gift, and my only treasure — a good, sharp knife I'd stolen from my father's workshop.

That night I rushed through the pot-scrubbing even more carelessly than usual, knowing the cook would be furious in the morning. I carried my box from the little chamber where the stillroom maid was already snoring (I'm not sure she ever noticed I was gone) and settled in on the pallet next to Meg's.

She wasn't there when I came in. I knew she often sat up late in the servants' hall, playing at dice, telling stories, exchanging household gossip. I didn't spend much time there myself. I was generally too tired, working as I did from dawn to nearly midnight, and I felt uneasy with my fellow servants. I'd never known myself to be shy, and I liked storytelling and dice-play as much as anyone, but somehow I never got on with the other servants. The men were a pack of greasy knaves, forever pinching and prodding the maids as if they were poultry on a market stall. And the maids seemed a giggling, simpering lot, who made far too much of the stupid servingmen for my liking. Only Meg stood apart, in my eyes a pearl among swine. Yet she mingled with them as an equal, and they liked her as they never did me.

So I lay awake, listening to the songs and laughter, waiting for Meg to come to bed. When she finally appeared I could see by the light of the candle she carried that she was flushed and giddy with too much wine.

She said she was pleased I'd come, that she knew I'd protect her from ghosts and bugbears, and that for the first night in four she felt safe enough to fall asleep. Which she promptly did, leaving me wide awake with an uneasiness I scarcely understood, mixed with delight at being so close to her, near enough to feel her warmth and hear her gentle breathing.

Her pallet was only a hand's breadth away from mine, and I felt myself sorely tempted to reach out and stroke her shoulder, or pass my fingers through her thick, curling hair. My desires surprised and shamed me — for lust was the one sin I'd thought myself free of. I had always scorned those fools who kissed or clipped or swooned and sighed. For I would as soon kiss a dead mackerel as kiss the boys who were my playfellows. And as to the girls, well, their mothers never let them near me, fearing I might infect them with my idleness and wicked ways.

But nevertheless, though the lust came late to me, it came with a vengeance. So I wrapped my arms tightly around myself, partly to keep my heart from leaping out of my bosom, partly to prevent my hands from straying.

I passed several nights this way, scarcely sleeping. As Meg grew more refreshed and rested, so I grew wearier; one waxed as the other waned. Finally, in the early hours of one morning, after a night of fitful sleep and puzzling dreams, I yielded to my desire. I reached across the space that separated us and began to caress her, lightly touching her face, her neck, her shoulders. She stirred and smiled in her sleep, gave a little sigh of what sounded like pleasure. I willed myself to keep my hands above her bedclothes, afraid she might waken, but half hoping she would. Forgetting myself, I leaned over and kissed her on the lips, and her eyes opened. She lay still for an instant, then sat upright, reached out and struck me a blow that knocked me halfway across the room.

Just then the majordomo rang the bell that called the kitchen servants to rise. Meg stared at me for a moment, then gathered up her clothing and ran from the room.

I struggled through the day, feeling like the boy in the old story who had a fox gnawing at his vitals. I turned the spit, scoured the cauldrons, scrubbed the grate in a trance, unaware if I was cuffed or cursed or even praised for my efforts. I was desperate to talk to her, felt I had to explain, beg forgiveness, but she never came near me all day long.

That night I was kept late at my labours. It was my lady's birthday, and there was a great banquet, with a company of players to entertain the guests. I was still scrubbing platters long after the others had retired to the servants' hall, to toast her ladyship's health in the wine she'd sent down to us.

I knew I'd have no rest that night if I didn't see Meg, and against my usual custom I resolved to join the revels in the servants' hall. They were all singing and carousing, but fell silent when I appeared, until one of the housemaids giggled, sending the rest of the company into fits of laughter. At the far end of the table I saw Meg, sitting on the coachman's knee, whispering into his ear and stroking the bulge in his breeches while his hand crept under her petticoats. Feeling my stomach heave, I ran from the room.

I vowed I'd never stay another night in that household. Blinded by tears, I stumbled through the passageways, desperate to put as much space as I could between myself and Meg. Suddenly I heard music and the sound of very different festivities. I blinked away my tears and saw I'd come to the great hall. I'd rarely seen it, and never when it was in use, for kitchen servants had no business there. But I had nothing to fear now, nothing to lose, so I opened the door and found myself behind a tapestry, with a slit that made a perfect spyhole.

The guests sat massed together at one end of the hall. I'd never seen such a splendid company: rich velvets slashed with shimmering silks, vast lace collars intricately worked, jewels that sparkled from ears and throats and fingers. It amazed me to think these gilded creatures were those the kitchen privily called "the jackals", who left us at the end of an evening with a mountain of greasy trenchers, gobbets of half-chewed meat, huge basins crammed with fouled and wasted food.

The players who entertained this company were birds of a coarser plumage: bold colours, cheap cloth, jewels that were clearly paint and paste. But they seemed so proud and strong and sure of themselves as they danced and strutted about the hall that I was dazzled.

I'd been to the playhouse a few times, sneaking in through a hole in the wall with my playfellows. We loved the fights, though we never listened to the speeches. But what I saw now was a very different spectacle, a curious admixture of verse and music. I scarcely understood a word of it: they might have been speaking Dutch for all I knew. Until, in a sudden silence, I heard a player say, "Brightness falls from the air. Queens have died young and fair."

Pondering this, I felt my burning anger cool into a softer, sadder melancholy, and I was comforted.

All at once, I knew what I was going to do. I stole back to my quarters, avoiding the servants' hall, and took the cloak and my precious knife from my wooden box. Then out the kitchen door, across the yard, and into the stables. The dogs and horses knew me — I stole food for them when I could — and kept silent. I climbed the ladder to the loft where the stable-boys lived, knowing they were all safely drunk with the other servants. I found what I needed: a shirt, breeches, a woollen cap, someone's thick jerkin cast off in expectation of a warm night's carousing.

I threw off my skirts with no regrets, and put on the stolen clothing. Then, almost as an afterthought, I took my knife and lopped off my hair to just below my ears. I wished I had a glass to see myself. I know I'd never felt better in my life.

The players had left their wagon in the stable mews. I climbed in, burrowed under a pile of painted cloths. A long time later they came out of the house, singing and laughing. They must have been well-fed and well-paid for their labours.

"We'll go as far as Tottenham tonight," I heard one say. "Then we can lie longer in the morning before we travel north."

I was off to be a player. I knew they'd have me. It was just a matter of choosing the right moment to present myself.

THOUGHT I'd be safest keeping myself hidden until we were well out of London. The last thing I wanted was to be discovered and returned to my lord's house in disgrace. So I lay as still as I could in my dusty hiding place, fighting back sneezes. The players spoke among themselves for a while, but soon fell silent. I suppose they were tired after their efforts, although compared to my own dreary labours theirs hardly seemed like work at all. Two of them, who must have been the chiefs of the company, began arguing in low voices about the route they were to travel, the actors' pay, the date of their return to London.

At long last we came to the inn at Tottenham. I decided to keep hidden for the night. In my innocence, I thought they'd be better disposed to grant favours first thing in the morning, which shows how little I knew about actors.

It was closer to noon than morning when they emerged, grey-faced and bleary-eyed. I sat awaiting them on top of their wagon. When they approached, warily, thinking they'd caught a thief in the act, I somersaulted down to the cobblestones, then circled their bemused leaders in a series of cartwheels. Still standing on my hands I approached the older of the two apparent chiefs, and asked him if he needed a strong, healthy boy to serve the company.

He laughed and shook his head, saying he was hard-pressed to pay his players, and there was nothing I could do for them. My capers and cartwheels were all very well, but they were serious actors of histories, comedies and tragedies, not jugglers and clowns.

I said I didn't want any pay and I'd beg or steal what I needed to feed myself. I'd seen how weary they were after their night's work, and wouldn't they like someone to carry their bags and boxes and bring them breakfast in the mornings. And what if sometimes they were late getting ready, with their public beginning to stamp and grow restless. I know such things happened; I'd seen players hissed at and pelted with eggs for keeping their spectators waiting. I could come out and keep the groundlings happy with headstands and capers, and if there were any eggs to be thrown they could throw them at me.

The players stood around me, laughing, and their leader stroked his beard and said the salary I'd asked for was the very sum he could afford to offer. But he thought he could manage to spare me the occasional crust of bread, since it wouldn't do to have me caught stealing and get the whole company hanged as thieves.

So our journey began, with me on top of the heap of bags and bundles. I'd never been outside London before, and every mile had its strange sights and wonders.

That afternoon we came to a market town, whose name I don't remember, and I thought what fools and bumpkins the people here must be, calling this place a town that could fit into a single street of Westminster. They all gaped at us as our wagon rumbled into the innyard and when I carried in the company's boxes there was a crowd of admiring dogs and children at my heels. I felt worldly-wise and very pleased with myself, as I helped hang the painted cloth that had served as my hiding place, and which I knew now to be the backdrop for our makeshift stage. The players were ready to begin at the promised time, and I must confess I was as much relieved as disappointed that there was no need for me to divert the groundlings first. The whole town was there to see us, and the play, a blood-soaked tragedy of ghosts and stabbings and revenge, delighted them. We took in enough money to put everyone in a sweet temper, and bought ourselves a fine feast of ale and mutton pies.

I decided this was the life I liked, and the Queen's navy would have to wait.

The next day we travelled to another place, even smaller than the first, and repeated our triumph. But on the third afternoon our luck changed. The warm summer weather deserted us, and we set up our stage in the yard of a mean, unwelcoming inn, buffeted by a cold wind and gusts of rain. The two leaders, Collins and Hodge, argued about cancelling the performance, but Collins pounded his fist on the table and said that it was the law of the theatre that a play once promised must go on. If Hodge couldn't endure a little rough weather he'd best go back to London and make himself useful raising money for the building of the new playhouse.

Foul weather or not, a crowd gathered to watch us. Just as the play was about to begin, Harry, the young actor who played the lady Bel Imperia, fell down the tavern stairs and ripped his gown all down the back. Hodge and Collins kicked and cursed him for a clumsy fool. He screamed abuse at them for bringing the company to such a tumbledown hovel, and the other players soon joined in the fray. I glanced out the door and saw the crowd outside growing chilly and restless.

"Davy!" someone shouted at me. (That was the name I had taken.) "Go out and keep them happy while we mend Bel Imperia's gown."

I'd always boasted that I was afraid of nothing — no wall was too high to climb, no game too dangerous. But when I found myself pushed onto the wooden platform before that mob of surly yokels, I felt terrified for the first time in my life. I did a few half-hearted leaps and somersaults, heard the jeering and hissing, felt my stomach churning with panic as I heard them bellow, "Give us our money back!" Mid-cartwheel I felt myself pelted with a shower of eggs and rotten fruit.

I exploded into a fit of choler. I flipped over into a handstand, stared out at the crowd from my upside-down vantage point, and began to tell them what I thought of them.

"You pack of country idiots with dung for brains and toadstool faces — you deserve to live in a god-forsaken midden-hole like this place. You're a blot on your own landscape and your village a jakes full of festering rubbish. If you came to London we'd think the Thames had flooded, there'd be so many warty toads and goggling fishes filling our streets.

"Your stupid faces and scabby flesh are living proof of the Seven Deadly Sins: you're black with avarice, swollen with pride, horned with envy, bloodied with wrath, snoring with sloth, bursting with gluttony, scaly with lust. That you should be so privileged as to receive a visit from us is a wonder, that we should be forced to earn our bread from the likes of you is a crime. We'd do better to play to your dogs and cats, whose understanding is no doubt greater than your own. Now either shut up and appreciate our efforts, or go home and sink back into your shitpiles!"

I jumped back to an upright position, turned away, presented my backside, and bombarded the crowd with a volley of farts.

The fury drained out of me, my head cleared, and I was thunderstruck when I realised what I'd said and done, until I turned round and found them all cheering, laughing and calling for more.

Then I heard the flourish of our solitary trumpet. The Spanish Tragedy was ready to begin.

THEY said I was the hero of the day, and that my flyting of the yokels would be long remembered. If I could do as well whenever they were late, they would have no more grief from restless audiences. The players plied me with wine until I was dizzy, fed me slabs of roast beef that tasted all the sweeter because someone other than I had turned the spit. We sang and caroused until far into the night, the quarrels of the day long mended and forgotten, except for Harry, whose torn costume had been the cause of it all, and who sulked in a corner. Then we staggered up to the two mean chambers we shared between us, and fell asleep in a drunken heap.

In the middle of the night I felt someone's arms around me, and shook myself awake. It was red-headed, snaggle-toothed Tom, who called himself a poet.

"Psst, Davy, don't move. It's only me, Tom, keeping you warm and saluting that fine, brave backside."

"Get away from me," I hissed.

"Don't be afraid, I'm not going to hurt you."

"Then move away."

"Don't tell me no one's ever shown any interest. A fine boy like you." He nuzzled my ear.

"You've got the wrong idea."

"It's an excellent idea. Why not try it?"

"I don't lust after men. I like women." (This, at least, was more honest than he knew.)

"How sad. A terrible waste. A lovely friend of mine, who's dead now, alas, used to say that he who loves not tobacco and boys is a fool."

"Well, give me some tobacco, then, and I'll only be half a fool."

"You're a witty flirt," he laughed, and reached between my legs. "Hell's teeth!" He drew his hand away as if he'd touched fire.

"Shut up!" I hissed.

He said nothing for a few minutes, just lay there laughing quietly to himself, then sat up and took me by the hand.

"Well, your secret, like your virtue, will be safe with me, my strange Davy. But come downstairs now and we'll rake up our landlord's fire and I shall initiate you into the mysteries of the tobacco pipe. There, at least, is a vice we can enjoy together."

TOM was true to his word, and he kept my secret. I had little fear of discovery. Except for the way I pissed there was no outward sign that I was anything but a sturdy, beardless boy. So I was careful about the times and places I relieved myself. As long as I kept my wits about me I was safe. Or so I believed.

But I was cursed, like all women, with the painful monthly reminder of my sex. A few nights before our return to London the pain came on me, and the wretched blood flowed more heavily than usual.

While the others were occupied with their wine and gossip round the fire, I went out to the stables to replace the blood-soaked rag with a fresh one. I was standing in a dark corner, hidden behind our wagon, when someone came in with a candle. Cursing, I struggled to truss up my breeches, and looked up to see Harry peering at me suspiciously.

There was little love between us. Before I'd come along he'd been the baby of the company, and the fact that he was a proper player and I no more than a clown and dogsbody made no difference to his jealousy.

"What are you doing?" he jeered. "Stealing from the properties box?"

"Taking a piss," I said. "What about you?"

"None of your business," he said, then by the light of his candle saw the bloody rag at my feet. "You've hurt yourself?"

I said nothing.

He moved his candle, saw my half-trussed breeches, then put the light close to my face and thrust his hand under my shirt.

"You're a wench!" he cried. "I knew there was something awry about you."

I felt myself heating up with the same fury that moved me to break the nose of the prentice who'd called me a girl.

"Whatever I am, I can beat the shit out of you!" I spat in his face, blew out the candle, leapt upon him and threw him to the floor.

He ran from the stable, screaming and cursing, and I knew the game was up.

Some of the players thought it was a great joke. Others were scandalized.

"A woman in men's clothing is an abomination."

"Now wait." Tom came to my defence. "We put men into women's clothing on the stage."

"But that," said another, "is because a real woman on the stage would be an obscenity."

Poet that he was, Tom spouted what must have been Latin and Greek to further his argument. Everyone shouted, quibbled and interrupted themselves. My exposure had turned into a logic-chopping disputation, and if it weren't for the fact that none of them took their eyes off me, I'd have thought they'd forgotten me altogether.

Finally I lost my temper, and screamed above the

din. "What does it matter if I'm man or woman? I can do anything that a boy can do!"

"Except have a stiff prick," jeered Harry.

"There are women jugglers among the gypsies," someone said. "And our Davy, or whatever she's called, has proved himself — or herself — a fine, flyting clown."

"I want to be a player!" I cried.

"Never!" stormed Hodge.

"Impossible!" thundered Collins. "Do you realise, you silly child, that if we let a woman on our stage the Lord Chamberlain would take away our licence!"

That seemed to settle it. I was furious that night, when they made me sleep alone in a separate chamber, as if the weeks I'd served them and been their comrade had never happened.

I knew that in the morning all of them, except Tom, would treat me in a different way than they had before, and I wouldn't stand for it. So I stole out of the inn at first light, and begged a ride in a farmer's wagon, carrying cages full of squawking chickens to their doom in London.

THAT was more than a year ago. And never in my life, before or since, have I been as happy as I was then, as a boy among the players. So I know my only salvation is to be changed into a man, for there's nothing in me that feels like a woman. I can labour and run and fight like a man. I'd sooner wear breeches than a skirt, and I've vowed never to put on petticoats again. I'll pay you well. I've saved up my money for many months and I can give you as much silver as you want, although if you're wise you won't ask how I've earned it. They say you're honest, as apothecaries go, and you may know a few tricks that others don't. So I put myself in your hands, and I ask for your help, else I'll go mad or die of desperation.

"IT'S impossible, of course," said my father. "The woman's a lunatic."

We'd sent her away, promising we'd consider her plea. I told her to come back the next evening for our answer. The air was still blue with her tobacco smoke, and Moll had sung loudly to herself as she left the shop, having tippled off three bottles of wine single-handed.

"Shall we tell her we can't help her? I wouldn't like to tease her hopes with false promises."

"Nonsense!" he retorted. "There are rich pickings here. She says she has plenty of money. The girl's clearly a thief. If I hadn't kept my eyes clapped on her all the while, I'd be counting the spoons now. Whatever money we take from her has been taken dishonestly from someone else, you can be sure."

"She seemed very trusting. It's a cruel thing to gull her."

"On the contrary. It's the only way to cure her

folly. We tell her it's a difficult task, with only a small chance of success, but we're willing to make the attempt to please her. Then we dose her with some harmless powders. We can keep her going for days or even weeks, until she comes to realise it's a futile effort. And meanwhile, we'll have plenty of meat on our table."

"Perhaps that's only half a lie," I said, yielding. "We're only promising to attempt it, not to accomplish it."

My scruples at least partly eased, I began to look forward to Moll's return. I lay awake very late that night, mulling over the story she'd told us. I found I was sorry I'd bidden her to wait until the next evening for her answer. I was impatient to see her again, and wished I'd told her to come back first thing in the morning.

I HAD persuaded my father to leave Moll's treatment entirely in my hands. Once he'd satisfied himself that I wasn't going to waste any expensive ingredients, he was content to return to his books. So I concocted an elixir full of herbs and spices that wouldn't do Moll any harm, might even be good for her, and tasted sufficiently nasty to let her know we meant business.

"God's teeth!" she spluttered after the first dose. "It's fire and brimstone."

"That's strong medicine. We're not just curing a headache," I reminded her, corking the bottle and locking it away.

"Aren't you going to give me the bottle?"

"I can't take the chance. This is dangerous stuff.

One drop too much and you might find yourself
metamorphosed into a hairy ape. A drop too little and
you might turn into a water-rat. We can't be too
careful. You'll have to come here and let me dose you,
once every day."

"How many days will it take?"

"That's difficult to say. Remember, there's no
certainty it will work at all. But you'll have to keep
going for at least a week or two before we can tell."

"That may be difficult," she said. "Sometimes my
business takes me far afield. I may have to miss a day or
two."

"Well, then, *caveat emptor*, and if you turn into a
mouse or a chicken don't come crying to me."

"I suppose I'll have to rearrange my affairs for a few
days."

"It depends how important this is to you. I'm not
forcing you . . ."

"I'll be back tomorrow at the same hour."

She left a cloud of tobacco smoke behind her.

¶ FOUND myself fidgeting impatiently all
day long, waiting for Moll. I'd hoped to persuade her
to stay and sup with us, or at least linger for a glass of
wine. But over the next few days it became her custom
to rush in, slap a coin down on the shop-board, grit her
teeth, swallow the mixture in one gulp and be off
again about her mysterious business.

One night she didn't come at all.

"I suppose the wench has come to her senses at last,"
my father said. "Never mind, we've eaten well for a
week. And the spring fever season's coming up soon."

I waited up half the night, listening for her knock at

the door, and passed all the following day in a foul temper. What an idiot she was, to imagine she could change her sex. And what a fool she was for wanting to. Then I began to worry: what if she lay sick somewhere, or injured? What if her unknown, unsavoury affairs had landed her in Newgate gaol? What if my own mixture, which I'd thought harmless, had poisoned her? And what difference did it make to me if it had?

By the next week, when no Moll had appeared, I'd given her up for lost. I was forced to admit that my interest in her had passed beyond the purely professional. And it was good to feel the old stirrings in my belly once again. For I'd thought that I was finished with such delights forever. When my sweet neighbour Jennet died, I'd vowed that Cupid's darts would nevermore pierce my scarred and armoured heart. At the age of seventeen, world-weary, I resolved to live loveless. Since then, of course, I'd had my passing fancies, but none that made me lose sleep or appetite. Until this roaring madcap Moll burst in upon me.

Then, late one night when I was damping down the fire, I heard a pounding at the shutters. I almost set the house alight, dropping a burning candle in my rush to unbar the door. It was Moll, sure enough, soaking wet.

"You're half-drowned. But it isn't raining."

"Let me in! Quick! They're after me!" She pushed me aside and dashed into the shop.

"You'll catch your death . . . Come upstairs. There's a fire in my chamber."

"Bolt the door, damn you!"

"There's a civil greeting. Don't worry, you'll be safe here." I shot the bolts, and moved a heavy chest against the door, just as a precaution. "Anyway, it will be easier for you to hide upstairs if anyone does come looking."

Once in my chamber, I helped her peel off her sodden clothes, and wrapped her in my warmest quilt.

"Sit closer to the fire. You can tell me what's happened when your teeth stop chattering."

I brought her a posset of hot wine mixed with strong spices.

"Now what's going on? And where were you last night?"

She gave me a dark look. "The places I go, and where I am when, are my own business, and I'll thank you to remember that."

"Your absence has led me to suppose you don't want any more treatments. We don't *need* your custom, you know."

"No! I want to be a man now, more than ever. I have to take my revenge on certain parties. I'm as strong as any two men now, but when I'm a proper man I'll have the strength of ten."

"That may or may not happen. But would it be impertinent of me to ask you why you're soaking wet on a dry night? Did you fall in the river?"

"Jumped in. I had to swim ashore."

"Ashore? Where were you?"

"On a merchantman heading for the Indies."

"The Indies!"

"I jumped ship."

"You didn't tell me you were going to the Indies."

"I didn't know myself. I was tricked. Some of my friends — or those I thought were my friends — carried me off to a fair over the river. They promised there'd be rich pickings — drunken revellers, fat purses, accidents happen. When we reached St

Katharine's Dock we stopped at the alehouse to have a drink and see the dancing bears. I thought I never tasted such foul ale in my life, but I realise now it was because it was drugged."

She broke off, peered at me suspiciously.

"Have you and your father sold any strong sleeping draughts of late?"

"Not for weeks. What happened next?"

"I don't know. I felt myself falling under the table. Now that's impossible, from one sup of ale as weak as baby's piss. I can outdrink anyone I know. I'm always the one who's left to carry home my fellows at the end of a merry evening."

"Never mind the bragging. Go on with your story."

She glared at me, but continued.

"The next thing I know, I'm belowdecks on a ship. My head was hammering, and I felt sick at my stomach, but I knew this was no drunkard's dream. I was tied hand and foot. So I mustered my strength, and began to shout, and I guess they heard me. Some sailors came running. They seemed as surprised to see me as I was surprised to be there, and they ran to fetch the captain at my bidding.

"Now his crew may have been innocent, but this fat, filthy pirate was in on the plot. He insisted he'd been paid good money by someone who claimed to be my uncle, and he was taking me to be a bonded servant to a merchant in the Indies. Now as you well know, I've had my bellyful of servanting, and if I choose to voyage to the ends of the earth it will be on my own terms and of my own free will. Whether it was in fact my uncle — the pious hypocrite — or only someone pretending to be him, I don't know. There are a few who would be pleased to see me gone from London. I asked the captain how much they'd paid him, and he told me twenty pounds. I said I'd give him twice that amount, which I had with me, if he'd set me free.

"He looked startled, then discomfited, to think I was carrying money on my person that he hadn't already discovered and stolen. But I had a horde of coins well-wrapped in cloth, so they wouldn't jingle, concealed in a secret pocket inside my doublet. So he had one of the sailors cut me free, and I duly produced a bag of coins, which he counted out, smacking his lips and chuckling.

" 'I'm grateful to you for your generosity,' he said, 'but alas we weighed anchor full half an hour ago. So I'm afraid we must abide by the original arrangement and carry you to the Indies, or feed you to the fishes if you grow troublesome.'

"If he anticipated the kick I aimed at his codpiece I might now be on my way to the Indies, or in the belly of a whale. But he never saw it coming, so dazzled was he by his newfound wealth that he was quite astonished and fell writhing to the floor. His sailors simply stood where they were, showing no inclination to help him. I think he must not have been a popular captain — he was no Sir Francis Drake in any case.

"So I bolted up the ladder and across the deck, leaped over the rail and swam for the bank. Some watermen pulled me ashore, but I scarcely paused to thank them. I started running, fearing the old pirate would be following hard behind, to punish me for the blow to his manhood. I never stopped till I came here."

"There's been no sound of pursuit," I reassured her, "and no pounding at the door. In any case, no merchant captain could afford the risk of missing a good tide, so I think you're safe."

"At least I'm warm and dry now."

"But forty pounds the poorer."

"None the poorer. All the coins were counterfeit. Newly minted and ready for distribution. That was my main intention in visiting the fair."

HER escape had tired her, and I helped her on with one of my nightsmocks, then tucked her into my bed under a pile of warm coverlets. She was fast asleep before I climbed in beside her. I lay awake watching her, looking out for any sign of a fever or chill. She never stirred, even when I began to caress her breasts, that had always been so well concealed beneath her doublet. I thought her a fool for ever scorning such fine, weighty mounds and preferring instead the flat and disappointing bosom of a man. Made bold by the sleeping draught I'd given her in the spiced wine, I unlaced the smock and licked the dark tips of them, that still tasted faintly of the river, then wrapped myself tightly about her lest she grow cold in the night, and finally fell asleep.

SOME noises in the street woke both of us. Moll opened her eyes, saw me, and started, as if surprised to find me there. It seemed she'd forgotten where she was and how she came to be there.

"Why did you come?" I asked her.

"I had to get away from those who would do me evil. When I came dripping from the river I thought first of your house, since no one knows of our connection."

"I'm honoured that you trust me."

"I do not trust you, mistress. I trust no one."

"Perhaps that's wise."

"I trust you so little, in fact, that I think you are cheating me with your elixir."

"What makes you think so?" I asked, all innocent, but inwardly quailing at the prospect of an irate Moll at large in my chamber.

"It isn't working."

"How do you know?" I stalled for time.

"See for yourself." And she leaped from the bed, thrusting off the smock I'd lent her. "Look!" she said, standing naked and furious before me. "What do you see?"

I looked. Long and leisurely. I saw a fine strong body, sturdy arms and legs, a welcoming bosom and a comfortable belly, with a thick bush of red-gold hair beneath it. I felt a sweet stab of pain in my own corresponding parts.

"I see a lovely woman."

She grew even angrier.

"And what *don't* you see?"

"I don't know what you mean."

"What's missing?"

"Absolutely nothing," I said warmly.

"Look closer!" she demanded, thrusting herself so near to me that her upstart nipples nearly put my eyes out.

"Believe me, Moll, I would gladly crawl inside your body and study you from the inside out, if it were possible — but I see nothing amiss."

"Look at my bosom!"

"I can scarce avoid it."

"Well, then, you can scarcely fail to notice that my breasts are as big as ever they were, and such hair as I have thereon is but a fine down, barely visible save in the strongest light."

"True."

"So when do those womanish dugs fall away? And where is my thick mat of hair that should grow in their place?"

"These things take time," I prevaricated.

"And consider these hips and flanks."

I did so, patting and stroking judiciously.

"All wide and curving."

"True." I measured them appreciately.

"When will they narrow?"

"Hard to say," I mused.

"And what about down below?" she demanded. "No sign of anything that would fill a codpiece!"

"Indeed not!" I agreed, considering the matter closely.

"Then what are you going to do about it?"

"What would you have me do?"

"Carry out your commission, and turn me into a man!"

"I've never heard such stupidity in all my days. I've heard your story, and I begin to know you a little, and yet for the life of me I cannot understand why you should wish to change your sex."

"Mark me well, apothecary, I dislike certain lectures first thing in the morning. And I do not pay you for your opinions, but for your skill. So double the dose, or whatever will make your elixir do its work, but do it fast, for I have no more time to waste."

"And what if I gave you all the drugs of Arabia and the poisons of Italy and the horns of unicorns powdered and the bones of dragons? I would grow fat and rich at your expense. I could try out new elixirs till doomsday."

"I will make myself a man! And if you do not

change me with your powders I shall find another pill-merchant who will."

"You won't, Moll. Mother Nature made you a woman, and a woman you must be."

"Mother Nature made a mistake."

"What sort of mistake?"

"Anyone as brave and strong as I am ought to be a man. Not a silly petticoated woman who bleeds and breeds and whimpers."

"For all your bold bravado, Moll, you're a silly child who knows nothing of life." I was so angry I almost struck her, then remembered in time that she could easily knock me senseless, so forebore, and simply drew her down into the bed again, for she shivered with cold and vexation. Such anger as she felt did not prevent her from clinging to me closely, for the chamber was freezing. Such anger as I felt did not prevent me from rubbing her back and shoulders, to make her warm again.

"They say alchemists know how to transform base metal into gold. Surely changing female to male is not so different."

I stopped rubbing. "Are you implying that woman is base metal, and man is gold?"

She grabbed my wrist, and then put my hand back on her back and made me rub again. "Indeed, the order of the world has made it so. Women are slaves and men are masters. And I, mighty Moll, the terror of Cheapside, the scourge of Southwark, am meant to be among them."

"You are as blind as you are foolish, Moll. What of Her Majesty? She's no slave, but the bravest, wisest, most glorious of princes — and still a woman. When she was young, you know, she bled every month as you and I do."

"Foul treason!" cried Moll. "Her Majesty never . . ."

"You've been mixing too much with men. The world is full of brave, strong women. If you're too stupid to see them, it's you loss, not mine."

I sat upright, and pulled the covers up around me.

She pulled the covers down again, and pulled me with them. "Even women think I'm a freak. They treat me like a two-headed calf. They'll have nothing to do with me."

"What about me?"

"You're an exception."

"Just another two-headed calf like you are, Moll. Well, if you looked farther than the end of your nose, you'd find a lot of us about. I promise you, Moll, you can be as bold and strong and free as you are now, and still be a woman, and the wisest of your sisters will love you for it."

"Love," she sighed, "is also part of the problem. For when I love, and when I lust, it's woman who's my object. Cruel Meg of the kitchen was not the only one who smote me so. There have been two or three others since, that have tempted me. They offer friendship, but I want something more. And when I have made this known to them, they shun my company, or laugh at me for a mad, moonstruck fool. Because I'm nothing to them without a stiff bull's pizzle and a pair of wobbling balls."

"The more fools they," I said, stroking her arm. "I think perhaps you have been unlucky in your choice of women. For there are those of us who know that such

45

machinery but gets in the way of a woman's true pleasure."

"I've never hungered after such toys myself," she avowed, letting her hand wander over my thigh. "But they seem to be needful." Her voice shook slightly. "I've never met a woman who wanted me without them."

"Now that proves it, Moll. You *are* a fool." I kissed her over and over again, then drew her close and taught her otherwise.

WHEN we finally came downstairs it was almost noon, and my father was clattering about the shop in a foul temper. It was his usual custom to lie abed until I brought him his breakfast, then dress at his leisure, browsing among his scrolls and notebooks while I unbolted the shutters and readied the shop for the day's trade. This morning, however, he'd had no breakfast, no time for rumination, and had been forced to rush into his clothes to answer an insistent battering at the door, which I'd heard nothing of. It was some silly lordling, come at dawn in urgent pursuit of an aphrodisiac. He'd blocked the whole street with his coach and horses, and the early morning traffic of carts and wagons had piled up behind it. There was an awful din of cursing wagoners, screaming fishwives, squawking chickens, all frantic to get to market before the prices dropped. Bleary-eyed, unbreakfasted, confused by the din and mystified by the presence of a heavy chest blockading the bolted door, my father took twice as long as he should have to prepare the mixture. Then, when the noble idiot departed, my father discovered he'd cheated himself soundly by asking half our usual price.

"Are you deaf, woman? Where in God's name have you been? Lying abed so late . . . Didn't you hear the din? Didn't you hear me calling you?"

Then he saw Moll, and fell silent.

"We were awake very late," I said. "Moll's had some trouble. She came here for safety."

"We're not innkeepers," he scowled, "and if you want sanctuary, try St Bride's church."

"I'm profoundly grateful for your hospitality." Moll bowed with a brave flourish. "If there is any service I can render you . . ."

He pulled himself up, remembering she was a customer.

"On the contrary. We should be serving you. Please forgive my short temper. I've been sorely tried this morning. Please partake of some breakfast, which I'm sure my Bridget will gladly prepare, before you swallow your elixir."

"I've decided not to continue with the elixir for the present," said Moll. "I'm resolved to try a new and different form of treatment."

"If there is anything we can supply . . ."

"I'll not hesitate to ask you," she said, grinning at me as she strode out the door.

$\mathcal{M}$Y father stood silent, stroking his beard, gazing at me thoughtfully. I hurried about the shop, tidying the mess he'd made in his haste to prepare the aphrodisiac for the impatient customer. Wherever I moved, I felt his eyes follow me.

Finally, after an hour's silence, he announced, "Our stock of dried roots and powders is very low."

"No matter," I said. "By next week we'll have our new supplies from my aunt in the country."

"I want you to go north and visit her."

"But the wagoner will deliver them sooner than I could get there and back. She's surely sent the cargo away by now."

"Never mind. It's time you learned something about the provenance of the plants we work with. A part of your instruction I've sadly neglected. And I think it would do you the world of good to have some time out of London. You can leave tomorrow morning. I'll arrange your transportation. And you needn't worry about me or the shop. I'll manage well enough for a few months."

I passed the rest of the day in a fever compounded of delight at what had happened between Moll and myself, and distress at having to go away. I'd tried, subtly, to convince my father that it was a bad time for a journey, that he needed me in the shop as the warm weather approached, with its fevers, lovers' quarrels, and fits of the green sickness. But he was adamant. He cast my horoscope to prove it was an auspicious time for a journey, and claimed he had money and messages for my aunt that could never be entrusted to the common carrier. He said he was puzzled that I should be so reluctant to go — I'd begged for years to be allowed to visit her.

At no time did he allude to Moll's overnight visit. But he knew what had happened. My father may have been worldly in some respects, but seeing Moll and me descending so cheerfully from my chamber, he was mathematical enough to put two and two together.

Moll had said nothing about returning. I cursed myself, for I should have made her promise to come back. Now I was in an agony of uncertainty: would she reappear when the spirit moved her? Would she come back at all? I know she liked our wanton morning, but would she see it as other than a fleeting pleasure?

By late afternoon I could endure it no longer, and went off in search of Moll, telling my father I was going to Cheapside to find some presents for my aunt. I remembered Moll saying she lodged at an alehouse in Chick Lane, and I hurried there with little hope of finding her. Moll was hardly one to spend the day keeping to her lodgings. She'd be abroad on some mysterious business, no doubt, but I could try to leave her a message.

Mother Bunch's alehouse was a black hole that smelled of piss. A rheumy-eyed old woman lounged in the doorway, a tobacco-pipe like Moll's clamped in her toothless jaw.

"We're closed," she said, looking me up and down.

"I'm looking for Moll."

"Moll who? I don't know any Moll. What makes you think you'll find her here?"

"She told me she lives here."

"What's she to you?"

"A friend."

"You don't look like any friend of Moll's I ever saw."

"It's important that I see her."

"She isn't here."

"When will she be back?"

"How should I know? Maybe tonight. Maybe next week. Maybe never."

"Can I leave her a message?"

"Please yourself."

"Will you remember to tell her that . . ."

"Me? What am I, her bleeding chambermaid? I've got beer to brew and barrels to fill and a tavern to run.

In two hours this place will be so full of swilling sots that if you died on the spot you'd have no room to fall down. And you want me to go memorising messages . . ."

Just then two small boys, dragging a third by the collar, rushed into the lane. They stopped in front of the alehouse and threw some pebbles at the wooden shutters above our heads.

"Moll! Hey Moll! It's us — we got him!"

The shutters opened, and Moll's voice bellowed, "Well, don't just stand there like a pair of ninnies! Bring him up!"

They ran past us, into the alehouse, dodging a kick from the old woman, who cursed them long and loud, then turned to me and said, "Like I told you, she isn't here."

I held out a coin. She bit it. Then I fished out several more. She thrust them into a pocket of her filthy apron.

"Up the stairs and turn right. But on your own head be it."

The stairs were little more than a rough ladder and I nearly broke my ankle on a board half rotted through. I heard shrieks and curses from a room across the narrow landing, and I opened the door to meet an extraordinary sight.

Moll stood in the centre of the room holding a little boy upside down by the ankles, shaking him vigorously.

"I don't have it!" he blubbered.

"He does!" The two boys who'd brought him stood at her side, their arms folded, smirking with satisfaction. Several little girls and boys sat on the floor or lounged on a rumpled pallet, jeering and giggling.

"We'll have no liars here!" Moll cried, and gave him another shake that made his teeth rattle. A shower of silver coins jingled onto the floor.

"Hidden in your shirt, just as I thought, you scabby little bastard!" She turned him rightside up, tucked his head under her arm, and began boxing his ears.

"Rule the first," she said, punctuating her words with a blow, "is never cheat on your comrades. Rule the second," another clout, "is never lie to a fellow thief. And rule the third," with a resounding smack, "is never, never get caught with the goods still on you. Now get out and don't let me see your ugly face here again until you've stolen enough coins to buy gingerbread for us all. Only then will we accept you back in the fold as a repentant sinner. Until then, fare thee well!"

She spun the snivelling child around and propelled him through the door with a kick up the backside. With her foot still in the air, she looked up to see me standing there.

"What in hell are you doing here?" she demanded, in a voice cold as ice.

"I have to talk to you."

"Get out!" She whirled through the room, hoisting up the children, who'd been sitting and staring at me with fascination. She hustled them out, slammed the door, then turned to face me.

"I don't like being followed. And I don't like being spied on. What I do with my time is my own affair and if I want you to know about it I'll tell you. Do you think you own me, because of what passed between us this morning?"

"I haven't come to spy. But I had to talk to you. I

just wanted you to know — my father's sending me away."

"What's that to do with me?"

"I wanted to see you before I go. It could be a long time . . ."

"What makes you think I'd care?"

I felt sick when she said that.

"I hoped you might."

"You hope too much."

"I think you're sorry I've found you here. You're ashamed, aren't you? You'd like me to think you're the queen of the thieves, when all you are is a wet-nurse to fledgling pickpockets." As I heard myself speak, I thought, you fool, hold your peace or you'll ruin everything. But some needle of vexation pricked me sorely, and it was as if some cold, spiteful stranger spoke from out my mouth. "So don't come the high and mighty one with me. You're just another coney as far as I'm concerned. Gullible enough to throw away good money on a trumped-up miracle cure to turn you into a man. Anyone with half their wits about them would know such things are impossible. You're as silly as the lovesick swains who plead for magic potions."

"So you cheated me."

"You cheated yourself. We never said we'd do anything but try."

"You took my money. I could happily run you through, and your fat father as well."

"You know yourself there wasn't a penny in your purse honestly come by. You ride on Fortune's wheel like everyone else — the cheater cheated, the robber robbed. And don't forget, you begged and pleaded for our elixir. We didn't force it on you."

"Get out of here before I wring your neck."

"Even with the marks of your love-bites still on it? Oh Moll, you do have a short memory."

She turned away. "Whatever memory I have of it has been spoiled now."

"That can't be true." I knew I should have held my peace.

"You *are* presumptuous, Bridget. You hardly know me."

"I know you better than you think."

"If that were true, you'd know enough not to come prying after me."

Part of me wanted to fling my arms about her and beg forgiveness; part of me wanted to fling my arms about her and throttle her.

"Would you have me sit spinning at home, pining like a captive princess for her knight to rescue her? Am I supposed to wait upon your pleasure, and hide myself away until it strikes your fancy to seek me out? If that's the case, you need no drug to transform you, Moll, for if you think thus, you're more than half a man already."

"I suppose you mean that as an insult. Well, I take it as a compliment. I'm not a peevish virgin who despises men as you do."

She knew that would cut me. It seemed even our short acquaintance had given us a fine awareness of each other's weak spots. I slammed the door behind me.

The next morning I set off on the journey to my aunt in Norfolk.

I LEFT London at first light, in the wagon that would take me to my aunt's village. There was only the wagoner and myself, and a cargo of paper for the press at Cambridge. The driver was a taciturn old man, and I was in no mood for conversation, any pleasure I might have taken in the adventure spoiled by the manner in which it had come about. I was angry at my father and I was furious at Moll. Yet every step the horses took me away from the city, and from her, stretched my heartstrings almost to breaking point.

We had reached Shoreditch when a sudden, terrible noise made us turn and look back towards the city: a great thunderous tolling of all the church bells in London. The sky grew black with crows and starlings disturbed from their nests in the steeples, and underneath the insistent clangour we could hear another sound, a rising murmur of wailing and lamentation. We sat in the wagon as if turned to stone, saying nothing, until a horseman thundered past us, his rich clothing all torn and dishevelled. Another rider followed, then another, who paused beside us long enough to cry, "The Queen is dead."

We drove on, the old wagoner and myself, both of us weeping. It was as if the sun had fallen from the heavens. All my life had been lived under Elizabeth's glorious reign, and the old man said though he remembered other sovereigns, there had never been a better one.

Between my private miseries and the public sorrow, seen on tear-stained faces in every village we passed through, the journey was grim. The weather reflected the universal gloom and turned cold and wet as November. So my arrival at my aunt's was not the cheerful family reunion it should have been.

I HAD only met my aunt once before, when she'd come to London after my mother died. But there was a strong affinity between us. My father said I was very like her. She supplied us with a stock of dried herbs and medicinal roots at regular intervals throughout the year, and my father sent her money with a trusted friend from their home village. With every cargo she sent me pots of jam, dried flowers and the most wonderful honey. I returned the favour by sending her needles, pins, glass bottles and bolts of fine cloth.

She lived at some distance from the village, in a small, snug cottage on the edge of the fens. You could look in any direction and see nothing but flatness, with a faraway church tower floating on the horizon like a ship at sea. It was an eerie, lonely land, with none but the birds for company.

When I arrived she brought me to a row of wicker-work hives behind her house and solemnly introduced me to her bees.

"I tell them all my important news," she said, "and that's why they give me such good honey. If you thank them for all the honey and beeswax I've sent you in London, they'll appreciate the courtesy and never sting you."

In spite of living far from her neighbours, she had many visitors. There were old women, who had known my father as a boy, who wanted news of him. Was it true he was a great wizard, who had lords and rich merchants consulting him? (I thought of the silly noble nitwit who'd come clamouring for an aphrodisiac the morning before I left.) Was it true he'd made a fortune through his skills as an apothecary? (I thought of the poor neighbours who brought us pies in exchange for powders, and then, like stepping barefoot on a hot coal, I thought of Moll.) Was it true there had been terrible omens and a dreadful tempest in London before the Queen died? (I could hardly confess that in those last days of Gloriana's reign my attention was occupied solely in listening for Moll's heavy tread across our threshold.) I didn't actually lie to them, but I satisfied their curiosity in a way that enhanced my father's reputation somewhat more than the bare facts justified. I'm sure he would have approved.

In addition to these callers, who came to see me as a curiosity, there was the never-ending procession of villagers asking for my aunt's help in curing ills, birthing children, persuading reluctant lovers, increasing wealth. As in London, most of the petitioners were women, with the same woes as their sisters in the city. But their troubles had a more rustic flavour:

"My cow isn't giving enough milk."

"Do you have any cure for hornets' stings?"

"The farmer tumbled me last Harvest Home and now he's turned me out because of my swollen belly."

"How can I keep the fox from stealing my hens?"

"My husband says the baby's a changeling."

"The butter won't come."

THERE were those who prescribe flogging as the only sure way to cure a lunatic. I think my father intended my exile as the same sort of salutary punishment, to purge me of my lust by a dose of rigorous country life. But his purposes were thwarted, because the time of separation only increased my love for Moll. Far from forgetting her, I thought about her every hour in the day, and suffered only when I remembered I meant nothing to her.

Still, it would be a lie to say my time in the country was unhappy. My aunt was a wise and witty woman, and if she sensed that something troubled me, she was tactful enough to keep from asking questions. Although her life had not been easy, I never met a more contented soul. She'd married young, but all her children died, and her husband went off to be a soldier. He must have been killed in the Low Countries, for she never heard more of him. Unlike my father, her younger brother, she never felt any need to leave her native place. Her only trouble, beyond the inevitable uncertainties of the weather and the harvest, was an ancient feud with a nearby farmer, who coveted her patch of land.

"He's a wild projector, who dreams of draining the fens, and wants to cover all the country round — even where my cottage stands and my garden grows — with a kingdom inhabited by none but his own cattle."

When my aunt was not busy dosing the neighbourhood with its pills and philtres, or helping women in childbed, we spent many days out gathering plants, fair weather or foul. I'd reckoned myself a good enough herbalist, but I began to realise how little I'd known. I made new discoveries every day, for my aunt was an enthusiastic and patient teacher. She loved and understood the earth she lived on, and knew the name and powers of every weed, every tree, every mushroom, every hidden root. She had a prodigious knowledge of healing and magic, and I realised that all my father's book-learning was but the thinnest gloss on what she'd taught him.

At night she'd ask me questions about London — what the people did to earn their bread, how they took their pleasures — and in return she'd tell me of the village and the country round about, remembering stories that old women had told her, which they, in turn, remembered from other old women long before. There were tales of bugbears and goblins that had terrorised the neighbourhood; phantom armies and ghost ships that sailed across the land; spirits of trees and water; Mother Earth, who needed to be placated before the crops grew, no matter what the priests and churchmen said about it.

Her bees were her greatest delight, and some weeks after my arrival they swarmed to a new hive she had ready for them, well-rubbed with lemon balm and fennel to draw them to it, with a piece of old honeycomb inside to welcome them home.

"The bees that swarm in May yield the best honey. In September you can help me gather it. Then we'll send you home at Christmas with some bottles of the sweetest mead you ever drank."

Christmas seemed a long time away, and by then Moll would surely have forgotten me. I resolved to return to London at the end of the summer, when my aunt sent her customary shipment of dried rose-hips, black bryony and other specifics for the ills of winter.

*O*NE morning, as we sat shelling peas on the bench outside the cottage door, my aunt squinted up at the sun, then asked me if I was unhappy.

"How could I be unhappy with you, sweet Aunt? In these few weeks you've grown as dear to me as ever my poor mother was."

"I'm pleased to hear it. But something is troubling you. Are you grown homesick for London?"

"I miss someone there." And I thought to myself, don't press me, darling Auntie, or you'll hear something you may not want to.

"Please trust me," she said, as if reading my mind. "It may help you to speak it out. Forgive my presumption, but I think I know your sickness. I've pined for a lost love once or twice myself, you know. Love wasn't born the day you were, strange to tell."

"Love? I'm not sure that's the name I'd put to it, for there's as much anger and sorrow and bitterness as there is love in it . . ."

"I hope no man has hurt you," she ventured.

"No man," I said.

"A woman, then?"

"And if I were to tell you that was so . . .?"

"There's others been that road before you. It's a well-known fact that woman's touch is sweeter."

"Well-known to whom?" I asked. "No one has ever spoken of it to me."

"An old story. It takes little wit to realise that women's joys are safest when kept secret."

"That's why my father sent me here," I confessed. "To part us."

"Small wonder," she replied. "You've been a faithful servant to him. I know my brother's faults. He likes his whims well catered for. He won't be pleased to see your attention wandering."

"This isn't the first time."

"But you were younger then?"

"And most circumspect. All he noticed, if he noticed anything at all, were two little maids laughing together behind the garden wall. He cared not what I did with my little leisure, as long as I was prompt to serve him, and studied hard to learn the craft he taught me."

"But this time it's different, is it?"

"This time *she's* different." And I told her of Moll, and how she had smitten me, then spurned me.

"A curious creature," said my aunt when I finished my tale, "and not the bosom friend your loving father would want for you. She sounds a little dangerous to me."

"She has more worth and wit than anyone I know!"

"I'll not deny this," said my aunt. "I know that London tolerates some strange folk that would quickly be driven out of any country village. There are those who think that a woman who takes a man's attire is fit for hanging. They say she's worse than a witch."

"Please don't misjudge her from my poor description."

"I'll wait until I meet her, then," promised my aunt, "for I am nothing if not broadminded."

"Alas, you'll never have the chance, for she has gone out of my life altogether."

"You'll find a better love to replace her, then. The world is full of fine women, if that be your preference."

By then our aprons were brimming full of tender peas, so we carried them into the house and never spoke more of it.

The wagoner who had carried me from London was making another journey to the city, so I gave him a letter for my father, along with some sacks of dried herbs and roots, and a few bottles of my aunt's remarkable elderflower wine. In the letter I said I was happy and well and hoped he was also, and told him I intended to come home in September. Perhaps the clean country air — or too much elderflower wine — had gone to my head, for I never thought to ask his permission to return.

Yet only a day or two after the wagon departed, the carrier was back again, depositing the same sacks and parcels we had given him in a heap before our door.

"I may starve for lack of trade," he said, "but I'm keeping to the country. I'll carry no goods to London until the summer's out. The news met me on the road — they're all dying of plague. Not a happy omen for the new King, God save him."

It speaks ill of my filial virtues, but I fretted feverishly over Moll's wellbeing before I gave thought to the health of my father. Yet I wept long and hard in my bed that night, convinced I would see neither of them again.

AFTER news of the plague spread round the countryside, a change came over the district. People kept themselves to themselves, glared suspiciously at each other and sometimes threw stones at strangers.

"Angel of Death!" they'd cry. "Keep away!"

We heard the high roads nearer London were crowded with frightened, starving wretches, driven from one village to the next.

My aunt still had her petitioners, asking for herbs and charms against the plague. But where once they would have lingered in her kitchen, telling her their own troubles and putting those of all the world to rights, now they hovered on the door-step, took what they'd come for, and hurried away.

In spite of the fair summer weather, the people kept to their houses, except when working in the fields and tending their animals. When necessity drove them out of their cottages they put as great a distance as they could between themselves and their neighbours, straining courtesy. When we walked abroad to gather roots and flowers we rarely saw anyone, but sometimes felt the presence of others, hidden behind a bush or crouched in the high grasses, watching, invisibly, as we passed by.

My aunt was unperturbed. "When the infection subsides, people will be themselves again. We were spared here during the last great visitation, and I hope we may be spared again." She tried to keep me from dwelling too much on what might be happening in London. I know she worried about my father, whom she doted on far more than he realised or deserved, but she put a brave face on it and stayed outwardly cheerful.

Until one morning, when I heard her cry out, and rushed out of the cottage to find her weeping and cursing before her ruined beehives, all overturned and smashed to pieces, with the bees all gone away.

"And so it begins again," she said. "Damn the evil man, who bides his time and acts in an evil season."

The attack on the hives, she confessed, was only the latest salvo in her long war with the rich farmer who wanted her land.

"He knows I won't sell it," she said, "so he's trying to drive me away. He's loath to bide his time and wait for me to die. He may be twenty years younger than I am, but he's fat and choleric, and I'll wager you a new green gown that I'll be here to walk over his grave."

Late that afternoon we had a visitor, a pale, sickly-looking woman I'd seen about the village, who slipped into the house furtively, as if she feared pursuit.

"What was it this time?" she asked my aunt.

"The hives."

"I heard him go out in the night," she sobbed, "and I knew something was up. But I could do nothing, Mary . . ."

"He's bided his time," said my aunt. "It's been full six months since he cut down my cherry trees."

"He always turns worse when summer comes. In the winter he's content to sit and drink and brood. Beating the children or climbing on top of me are the only exertions he permits himself. But now, with the warm weather, he thinks only of his beasts and his land and how to increase them. I'm sorry. You know I would have warned you if I could."

"You do what you can," my aunt consoled her.

"He doesn't tell me anything any more."

"He doesn't trust you, any more than you do him."

"And I think he suspects about that last baby. He wonders how I could give him seven healthy children and lose the eighth. He says that among his cattle the proven breeders never miscarry."

"And is that what you are to him," I asked from my seat in the chimney corner, "part of his herd?"

"He says the more sons I give him, the fewer labourers he needs to hire. And even a daughter can be a sound venture, if she's put to a useful match."

"If you bear another it may well kill you," warned my aunt. "Look at her, Bridget, she's scarcely older than you are — not yet five-and-twenty."

I tried, out of courtesy, to hide my surprise, for I'd thought the woman closer to my aunt's age than my own.

"My first came when I was fifteen," she said. "And since then I scarcely remember a time when I wasn't carrying or suckling a new one. And now my husband has conceived of a new way to profit. He bids me hire myself out when next I have milk, to wet-nurse the babes of gentlemen. I'm growing tired. He seems to know my seasons as well as he does his milch cows', and at such times there's no putting him off. I've tried getting him drunk at suppertime, which sometimes stops him. But alas for all my efforts, it's happened again."

My aunt looked at her belly. "How far along?"

"Not yet three months. But there's no mistaking it. And I promise you, Mary, I'd rather die than bear it, after my sufferings with the last two. I know you've warned me against it, and I've told him the dangers, but he says I'm a foolish goose who doesn't know her own strength."

"So you want me to help you get rid of it."

"I can hardly bear to ask you, it seems such a brazen thing to come here begging for your help after what he's done to you."

"No matter," said my aunt. "In spite of what the old parson mumbled when he tied you and that brute together, you and he are not one flesh. He is my enemy, not his wife. And I hate to say it, but I venture that he's your enemy as well."

"I'm sorry about your bees. I'll try to keep watch, and warn you of his next attack if I can."

My aunt wrapped up some herbs and dried berries in a cloth. "Seethe these in water for an hour, and drink two ladles-ful. Do the same tomorrow, morning and night, and by the following day everything should be over. It will be easier this time than last, for you've come to me soon enough."

"Last time I hesitated far too long. Now there's no question." She left as secretively as she'd come, peering out the door to make sure no one was passing by, before she slipped away.

My aunt said very little for the rest of the evening. She mourned her bees, suspecting that the farmer had not only broken up their hives, but driven them in a swarm to his own land. "Where he'll use them cruelly, and they'll die. I'm sick and tired. I fear I'm too old for these struggles."

The next morning my aunt's spirits had lifted, and she seemed ready for, indeed almost relishing, a fray. "We'll have to keep a careful eye on the hens," she said, "but I think the cow is safe enough, with her byre so close to the kitchen. And one thing we must do before the day is out, is dampen the roof thatch with lime-and-water. The weather's dry, and I wouldn't put it past him to come upon us in the dark and set my roof afire. In any case, feud or no feud, it needs to be done at this season."

She bustled about all morning, hoisting up buckets full of water from her well, and mixing it with lime.

"Now, Bridget, you can help. Climb up the ladder, and I'll hand you up a bucket. Then you can fling the water about, until the thatch is well soaked."

It seemed such a sensible idea, and my aunt made it sound so simple, that I thought nothing of the difficulties it might entail until later that day, when I found myself clinging for dear life to a rickety ladder, my skirts tucked up to my waist, juggling a brimming bucket.

"I haven't much stomach for heights," I quavered as I climbed.

"Nonsense! Get up there! I've done this every year for thirty years in the dry season, all by myself, with no one to help me."

"You, dear Aunt Mary, probably flew up here on your broomstick."

"Hush!" she laughed, and rattled the ladder to give me a fright.

After several slips and false starts, I managed to climb to the roof, fling out the lime-water, succeeding — after one mishap — to get more over the thatch than over myself. When the bucket was empty I'd climb half-way down the ladder, hand the empty pail to my aunt, take the full one she held up to me, and climb back onto the roof while she refilled the first bucket from her great cauldron of lime-and-water.

We'd been at this for hours, moving the ladder around the house so I could reach all parts of the roof, when my aunt said that she was satisfied the thatch was now too damp to blaze up.

"It will be safe enough for a few weeks. We'll do it again later in the summer. Just toss this last bucket over the gable and you can come down."

Exhausted, I made one last climb to the top, splashed the mixture out of the bucket, and looked down at the garden below. I saw something move behind a thick clump of bushes, and froze in terror, thinking it was the evil farmer come to spy our our defences.

The lurking shape emerged from the bushes, and my aunt wheeled sharply at the sound of footsteps. I almost fell to my death when I saw the intruder was, unbelievably, Moll.

How I reached the ground in one piece I'll never know, but in an instant we were wrapped in each other's arms.

For a long time I couldn't speak. Perhaps I'd fallen from the roof, landed on my head, and this was all a fevered dream. But Moll looked real enough, felt real enough, and certainly smelled real enough. Dizzy with amazement, confusion, puzzlement, delight, I could barely gasp out the question, "How . . .?"

My aunt stood, spellbound, intrigued by this androgynous creature who, whatever else it was, was clearly no agent of the greedy farmer. Finally she bestirred herself. "Bring your friend into the house," she ordered. "We could all use a drink."

"I suppose you want to know how I cam here," said Moll, devouring her fourth piece of bread and cheese and savouring another glass of elderflower wine.

"I was curious," I said coolly, struggling to contain myself.

"Well, I went and asked your father where you were."

"But he sent me here to get me away from you. He'd never tell you."

"He did, though. All it took was a little encouragement."

"Encouragement?"

"I brought two friends with me when I came calling. Very interested in alchemy and conjuring they were. Took a good long look at all his manuscripts and instruments. Clumsy lads, though, dropping a couple of bottles, spilling a few elixirs, tearing the pages from a few books. He was reticent at first, of course, but seeing as my comrades were what you might call kindred spirits — ready to tear the shop apart in their eagerness to learn more of his craft — your father soon told me what I wanted to know."

I laughed to think of my father, outraged and spluttering.

"But how did you get out of London? They say the city is virtually sealed off by the sickness, and those who venture into villages beyond the suburbs are driven back the way they came."

"Oh, I left London before the plague appeared.

Some two or three weeks after you did, at most."

"You mean you came after me?"

"Well, yes and no. I decided it would be a good idea to get out of London for a time. You remember those so-called friends of mine who had me kidnapped? Well, I tracked them down and expressed my dissatisfaction. Then I decided I'd better travel for my health into the country, lest *their* friends decide to do the same thing to me. So I thought I'd find out your whereabouts and call in."

"It's taken you long enough. I've been here for months."

"Well, I might have come sooner. But there were some unexpected detours and distractions along the way."

"What manner of distractions?" I asked suspiciously.

"My throat's getting dry," she said, "and I'm growing weary. But if your aunt would kindly consent to open another bottle of her miraculous wine I may find the strength to tell you of my travels."

My aunt uncorked the bottle and filled our cups as Moll began her story.

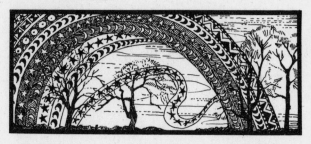

*Moll's Tale*     AFTER the Queen died, all London fell into a state of blackest mourning. The streets filled with weeping people, who'd come from all parts of the kingdom to bid her farewell. The taverns and ordinaries were fuller than ever, but strangely silent, and no jugglers, acrobats or ballad-singers had the will or the welcome to ply their trades. Even the nips and foists forebore from thieving, in spite of the rich pickings to be had among the gathering crowds. We may be thieves but we're loyal withal, and we loved Her Majesty as well as any City merchant or fat cleric ever did. I brought my young scholars down to the river to watch the funeral barge pass by, and if I'd caught any of them dipping their hand in a purse that day I'd have cut their fingers off.

As I said, it seemed a good idea for me to leave London for a time, so I joined the stream of country people heading homewards after their sorrowful pilgrimage to mourn the Queen. I had hoped to find a crew of players to travel with. There are some now who'd carry me with them for the sport of it; they don't all share the scruples of Collins and Hodge. But a season of grief is a profitless time for travelling players, and none of the companies stirred from London.

So I set off alone, which some would have considered foolish. There is little love lost between our bank of city tricksters and the ragged brotherhood of country vagabonds. If ever they venture into London and the liberties we gull them just the same as any other rural coney up for term-time, and why not — for anyone who lives too long among the sheep begins to think like one. Equally, if any of us from the town find ourselves waylaid by rural rogues and ruffians, we are robbed and beaten like any other unwary traveller. This state of affairs grieves me, and I would have it otherwise, for I think our two tribes would have much to gain from an alliance.

But you well know that I'm afraid of no mortal man and I had no doubt that I could take care of myself in the countryside. My strange appearance, which sometimes lands me in trouble, can also be a strong advantage: these bumpkins don't know what I am or how to place me, and by the time they've scratched their heads and pondered on it, I've got the better of them and moved on.

The first night of my travels I came to sleep at a well-known resort of outlaw wanderers, the great barn at the place called Draw the Pudding Out of the Fire. Here I found a company of forty or fifty people bedding down for the night: horse-thieves tethering their latest prizes; an Abram-man, who gathers alms by feigning madness, and his friend the dummerer, who earns his bread by pretending to be a poor mute (and who kept us amused for hours with his bawdy stories). There were a number of Irish beggars, who painted on their sores and scabs before retiring, so the weals and scabs would fade and look natural by daylight. There were a dozen or more wandering women, morts and doxies, who made up beds of straw for their men and themselves. They seemed a fair and spirited lot, and I would willingly have crawled in beside some of them, except, alas, each one had a rogue to roger her. Presiding over this cheerful company were several upright-men, who are like the kings of thieves, and have the right to take away any humbler rogue's booty, as the Crown takes the wealth of more honest citizens in the form of taxes. These kinglets can choose as they will among the women.

A little apart from this noisy crew there lay four young whores and their bawd, an old woman whose name I didn't know, but whose face I'd seen about the city. She told me she was starting on her yearly circuit of fairs and markets. Unlike the travelling players, she had no fear that the Queen's death would keep her customers away. She was very vexed at being compelled to pass the night in this place. It was her usual custom, on the first night of her travels, to lodge her wagon-load of women at a certain inn near Harrow. But this year, when they arrived there, they were told the old owner had died, and his successor didn't welcome such trade as theirs.

"Things are changing," she said. "There's a gloomy spirit abroad in the land, and it's not just the Queen's death either. People with sour looks and pious platitudes striving to prevent other folk taking their

pleasure. It doesn't augur well for the future. I'm glad I'm old."

Just then there was a commotion, when a pair of upright-men came in and kicked two lesser thieves away from their doxies. The supplanted lovers cursed and muttered, but it was the law of their tribe and there was nothing they could do about it. Until one of them remembered the party of unclaimed women across the barn.

They came over to our corner, and unceremoniously laid themselves down beside two of the whores, who leaped up and ran to their bawd.

"These fruits are not for the picking," she said.

"They're yours only if you pay my fee."

"We'll pay no fee," they said. "Whatever we find in this place is ours for the taking."

"Until the big, bad upright-man relieves you of it," I said to myself.

"We'll have them," one cried, seizing his chosen whore by the petticoat.

"You won't unless you pay the price," scolded the old woman, standing her ground.

"All you'll get from us, dragon, is a kick in the belly, with a dose of the pox for your girls as a free gratuity."

So engrossed were they in arguing with the bawd that they didn't notice me slip behind them, bearing my stout staff, with which I cracked both their pates with a single, mighty blow. They fell silently into the straw, their mishap unnoticed by their comrades, who either snored in a drunken stupor or merrily made the beast with two backs, oblivious to their neighbours.

"I think you'd do better to pass the night in your wagon," I told the women. "It's colder comfort than beds in an inn, but the night is mild enough, and you'll likely be safer outside than here."

The old procuress and her charges couldn't thank me enough, and pressed me to join them, fearing for my safety when the two brutes came to their senses. I told them I had nothing to fear, but that it would be my pleasure to bear them company. So we drove the wagon some distance away and made camp in an orchard. We all curled up together, with the whores' bundles as our pillows. All in all, my first night on the road was far sweeter than I'd ever anticipated.

The next morning, the old woman begged me to travel with them, as friend and protector. They'd feed me out of their own provisions, and their wagon, heavy-laden though it was, would carry me farther than I could walk.

I said I would not keep with them for the whole of their time in the country, for I had other plans, but I would happily travel with them for a few weeks along the way.

So for a while I entered into the role of chaperone and bodyguard to a bawdyhouse on wheels. Mother Appellina, the mistress of this establishment, had the calendars of all the major fairs and market days of England engraved on her memory, and over the years she had devised a convenient itinerary, taking in those places likely to assure the maximum profit. She had a store of advice about the routes she travelled: "Chipping Camden the night *before* the wool sales only. Afterwards, the Cotswold farmers trundle home like sheep to their own folds . . ." "Avoid Norwich, they're all bum-boys." . . . "Make Yorkshiremen pay double. They've great staying power." And so forth.

Our routine was the same in every place we visited. We'd arrive at the fairground or market early enough to choose a good site, and Appellina would set off with a bag of coins concealed in her bosom, to placate the local magistrates and obtain whatever licence was necessary. Meanwhile, the rest of us would erect the flimsy network of booths and tents that served as trugging-place. Then the whores retired to repair the ravages of travel and paint their faces. When Appellina returned, we would open for business. It was my task to collect the money from the ever-increasing stream of customers, while Appellina patrolled the booths to make sure no client overstayed his time. We worked long hours and were busy from morning until night. I sometimes grew weary of standing taking money, and thought how much wearier the harlots must be, sweating away in the tents behind me. I began to understand why Mother

Appellina travelled every year with a new crop of girls.

Sometimes I'd be summoned back into the booths to haul out a drunkard, or deal with some contentious coxcomb who demanded more — or different — than he'd paid for. But no matter how wild the altercation, or how loud the girl's cry for help, I was not to desert my post until Mother Appellina came to replace me by the money-box.

After one such fray, when a drunken customer demanded his money back because his own belly-full of strong cider had rendered him impotent, I returned from casting him into a nearby pigs' pen to find Appellina deep in conference with a bejewelled little rooster of a man, whose rich cloak and ruby earring contrasted sharply with a face that resembled the goats on sale across the market.

"Ah, Moll," said Appellina, beaming, "here you are. This gentleman has a most interesting proposition to make."

I didn't like the look of him. I lit my pipe and waited.

"He thinks you're a most remarkable creature,"

"Most remarkable," my admirer echoed.

"He is greatly taken with your appearance."

"Greatly taken," he agreed.

"Your curious mixture of masculine and feminine excites anew his jaded appetite."

"Jaded," he sighed.

"Withal, he has offered a most generous contribution to our funds in return for the privilege of escorting you to his magnificent residence so he may bed you."

"Bed you," he simpered.

"Tell him to quench his ardour up a donkey's

arsehole," I replied, and spat a great gobbet of tobacco juice on the polished toe of his scarlet boot.

"Why, Moll," cried Appellina, "I never thought such a bold adventurer as yourself would refuse an offer that promises both sport and profit."

"If I want anything from a man," I said, "I'll either ask him for it, pay him for it, or batter him over the head for it. Why should I play the whore for any man, when I can make any do my bidding? So there's an end to it."

Appellina and my thwarted gallant exchanged a rueful look, but he pressed a gold coin into her palm and bent low over her hand in what I suppose he believed to be an elegant bow. Then he sidled away.

Appellina, with her arms akimbo, shook her head and clucked at my stupidity. Then her infallible inner clock told her that a pair of young apprentices were about to overstay their hired welcome, and she rushed back into the tents to hurry them back into their breeches.

Relations between us were cool for the rest of the day, although admittedly there was little time for conversation, since business was brisk and she spent most of her time behind the scenes, encouraging the girls to despatch their clients with greater speed.

Indeed so busy was I taking coins into the coffer, and bidding the randy rustics to wait patiently until their turn was served, that I scarcely noticed the afternoon darken into evening. But finally even the local lechers had to stop for their suppers, and the impatient queue of customers had dwindled to a trickle, with all those wanting a tumble speedily serviced.

Then, from the back of the tents, there came a girl's scream, a scuffle, and Appellina's shout, "Ho, Moll!"

As per orders, I stood at my post until she rushed out, breathless, to guard the money-box.

"In the last booth," she panted, "and he's a wicked one. Nearly pulled poor Audrey's hair from her head."

Grabbing my staff I rushed into the booth, pushed aside the curtain, and found, to my puzzlement, no one.

I had scarcely time to ponder this when a thundering blow on my head knocked me to the ground, and I felt someone busy with a rope around my ankles, as another brain-cracking clout knocked me senseless altogether.

I might have been dead, for all I knew, until a great torrent of icy water crashed over me, and I realised I had to be alive, since it is fiery heat, not cold, that I expect to meet on the far side of the churchyard.

I found myself lying on a great, carved bed, now rather damp, in a chamber crammed full of tapestries, elaborate furnishings, dressers weighted with silver plate, heaps of painted cloths, golden candlesticks, statues, even an empty suit of brightly burnished armour. And peering out of this clutter, my goatish gallant of the marketplace, holding a silver water-jug.

"Good evening to you, madam." He bowed, a little unsteadily, with a sweeping flourish that almost threw him off balance. He was drunk.

"I've taken such a liking to you, in spite of — nay, perhaps because of — your rebuff to me this afternoon, that I thought it was only fair to offer you a second chance."

"A second chance at what," I growled, my head still throbbing.

"At sampling my amatory artistry; at enjoying the hospitality of my bed and my household; at having me your patron and protector."

"Now as then my answer remains. No upon no upon no. Are you such a booby you don't understand plain English speech?" I tried to rise, found myself still giddy from the blow that had flattened me, knew I'd have to buy time until I got my strength back.

"I bethought myself that as a remarkable personage, you might feel that I, accosting you in the public marketplace, was merely a member of the common herd. So I thought an invitation to my house would convince you that I am no seedy peasant, but a gentleman of substance."

"Invitation? Abduction, rather. Do you always woo your fancy with a blow on the head?"

"An unfortunate accident — an overzealous servant . . ."

"To be sure."

"But how otherwise to present a jewel than in its own true setting?"

I looked around. Everything in the crowded chamber was bright and shining and brand new. The wood still smelt of the joiner's workshop.

"Is this your shop?" I enquired politely, thinking him to be some sort of prosperous furniture-maker.

"Shop? What shop? A base insult! I am a gentleman of property, the richest in this town. My father, rest his soul, who died last Christmas, held the patent for all the salt sold in this county. A few words in the right ears, a few gifts in the proper pockets, and there was no sprinkling of salt on an egg or a pasty that he didn't have the taxing of. If he'd been able to fix it, we'd have set a tithe on all the salt in labourers' sweat and children's tears as well — for salt is a precious resource in this inland place, and those who squander it by spilling it out of their faces and onto the earth should pay compensation for such waste to the holder of the patent."

"And that patent-holder is you?"

"No, alas, for the holding was only for his lifetime. But my father was no fool, and put his fortune into land. So all I need to do is sell a few sheep, raise a few rents, or dispose of some acres, and I can furnish a chamber, or hold a great banquet, or purchase the cloaks and collars befitting a gentleman of my standing. How do you like these tapestries, newly come from France? That silver plate was made by the finest silversmith in London. One spoon of my cutlery costs as much as ten of the Lord Mayor's. That curiously-wrought bed you're resting on, with its allegorical pictures of Leda and the Swan, was done by a Flemish carver of great renown, whom I carried here especially from the Low Countries to execute the commission. The coverlet, with its pattern of all the flowers found in the Lord Chancellor's own garden, was embroidered by six maidens working night and day for fourteen months. It should have been completed in a year, but their eyesight began to fail. Later, I'll show you the staircase of porphyry and marble that leads up from the entrance hall (whose new wainscoting will be finished next month) to the long gallery that adjoins this chamber, wherein a Dutch painter is producing portraits of my ancestors to adorn the walls. As you can see, I am rapidly elevating this house to new glories, and our family as well, for I'm negotiating my marriage with the only daughter of an earl. She's ugly as the devil, but she's the sole heir, which makes her a pretty sight to me."

"Who does the armour belong to?" I asked.

"It was worn by my ancient ancestor, who came over from France with the Norman king."

"But it shines so. It looks brand new."

"That's because it has magic powers, conferred upon it by the wizard Merlin."

"You must be proud of it," I said, recognising it as the product of an Aldersgate tinsmith, who made cheap suits exactly like it for the playhouses.

"And now that I've persuaded you that I'm no common swain, perhaps you'll look with greater kindness on my suit for your favours?"

"Uncommon swain indeed," I said. "Come lie down beside me."

He leaped onto the bed, and untied the ropes that bound my wrists and ankles.

"Allow me to remove your boots, and my own also," I said, rising, "for the sake of the maidens' fine embroidered coverlet."

"A creature after my own heart," he purred, "who knows the true value of fine things."

I stood at the foot of the bed, tugging at his boot, with its high heels and silver spurs.

"A tight fit," I observed, panting, as I succeeded in pulling them off. "Your feet are over-large for these elegant boots."

"They say the size of the foot tells the size of the tool," he smirked, untrussing his breeches.

"We'll soon find out," I leered, tugging off his breeches with a flourish, and tossing them merrily across the room, where they upset a three-branched candelabra, just as I'd intended. The burning candles fell against a garish painted cloth, whose scene of Europa and the Bull soon blazed merrily, while the fire spread to the tapestries, but not before his breeches were all consumed.

"Fire!" he screamed.

"Oh, how clumsy of me!"

"Water!" he cried, leaping up in his shirt.

He rushed, bare-arsed, about the room, trying to beat out the flames, thrusting his head out of the door crying, "Fire in the upper chamber! Buckets! Water! Hurry, you idiots!" and returned to struggle with the flames anew.

I pushed open the latticework windows, climbed out on to the sill, knowing from what he'd said it was but a one-storey drop to the ground.

"So much for burning passions!" I cried as I jumped. But I doubt he even heard my execrable jest, so busy was he in saving his worldly goods.

I found myself in a muddy lane, and hurried away. I considered paying a visit to Appellina, to express my dissatisfaction at her part in the plot. Yet, in the end I thought better of it, wanting nothing more than to leave that wretched town as quickly as possible, lest I be charged with fire-raising.

I regretted having served as such a trusty watchdog over the old bawd's money-box, only helping myself to an occasional coin when the coast was clear. I'd always vowed I'd never steal from a woman, but I'm sorry I didn't make an exception in Appellina's case, for that old panderess stole from her women every day, and cheated them far more sorely than ever I could do.

I WANDERED the roads alone for a time, keeping out of the towns as much as possible, except for quick forays to cut a purse or two, that would find me the price of bread and a new tobacco-pipe. But otherwise, I kept to the highroads, sleeping in barns or under bushes.

My travels with Appellina and her whores had carried me farther north than I'd intended, and I discovered I was a long way from Cambridge, which I knew I had to pass before I'd find your aunt's village. But I'd heard from other travellers on the road that there was plague in London and I thought it was wise to keep to the north. Yet I had little liking for my own company after a fortnight's solitary wandering.

Then, one foggy day, as I walked gloomily along the high road, kicking a stone, I heard a curious jingling noise behind me, like a thousand tiny bells. I thought for a moment that I was hearing the music of the fairy-folk, which would surely send me into an enchanted sleep for an hundred years. It's said such things often happen to travellers in those wild parts of the country.

Then I looked over my shoulder and saw a line of people coming out of the mist. There must have been two dozen of them, men, women and children, and as they approached through the fog I could see their fantastical clothes, all patched and tattered, their golden caps atop faces that were either swarthy or painted eerily in reds and yellows. Behind them came three sway-backed horses and a mule, laden down with sacks and bundles. The mule bore a pair of pannier-baskets carrying what seemed like a heap of pumpkins, until a closer look revealed it to be a tightly-packed cargo of infants and small children.

I turned and waited for them to overtake me, but they stopped a few yards away and stared at me in silence. We stood thus for a long time — each side transfixed by the other's strangeness. Then I realised what I'd met — no horde of elfin dancers ready to drag me underground to serve their fairy queen, but a band of those wanderers who roam the shires and claim no place as their home, who some, sneering, call the Moon Men, and who themselves call Egyptians.

If I had found an explanation for them, they'd discovered none for me. I saw them whisper among themselves, debating, as others had before them, whether I was woman or man, lunatic or rogue. Feeling so many pairs of eyes upon me inspired me to perform, so I treated them to a display of the same capers and headstands that so pleased the crowds when I travelled with the players.

When I finished, they whistled and clapped their approval, and one of them came forward to offer me a drink of wine from a leather flask. Then I saw that the jingling noise that had preceded them came from the hundreds of tiny bells that hung about their garments, which themselves were a riotous mixture of old rags and rich fabrics heaped up together, with the old, worn clothes covering the new.

Then, as if to return the courtesy, some half-a-dozen broke forth from the crowd, shaking tambourines, leaping in a wild and merry dance. When they finished I shouted my appreciation, and to show I was no miser, offered them a lump of hard cheese, which was all I had that would answer to their wine.

They laughed and refused my offer with the gentlest good manners. They told me they were on their way to a rendezvous with another band of their own people, and if I cared to walk along with them I would find myself a welcome guest at the feast.

It startled me to find they spoke our language, so wild was their appearance that I thought they'd only babble in some moorish gibberish. They did indeed have their own tongue, and to my surprise they knew our thieves' jargon that we keep, country and city rogues alike, as the mark of our tribes. But they spoke good, plain English as well, albeit with an accent that was like the Irish and the Welsh and something strange all mingled together.

After a little while we left the road, and crossed through fields and woodlands until we reached the bank of a stream, where several dozen of these Egyptians were already encamped. When our party arrived there were shouts of welcome and warm embraces, and a frenzy of foreign gabble, with some pointing in my direction.

One old man, with twirling black mustachios, appointed himself my guide, and carried me about the camp, presenting me to his fellows.

I saw a group of women standing in a tight circle, facing inwards, flapping their petticoats and laughing at something inside the ring.

"They're preparing our dinner," explained my companion. But their circle dance was like no cooking I ever saw, and I drew closer for a better look. Inside the circle, two women were chasing a great, fat gander. Wherever he bolted, the women in the circle shook their skirts to drive him back into the centre of the ring. Finally he tired, and one of his pursuers swiftly throttled him. The whole crowd of them swooped down to pluck the bird and make it ready for the pot.

I asked why they made such sport of killing the bird, and my guide explained.

"That bird was a gift whose donor hasn't yet discovered he's given it. Should any passer-by happen upon our camp it would be most unfortunate if he discovered us killing his neighbour's goose. So the women stand in a tight circle, and the deed is done behind their skirts."

"Do you steal all you eat?"

"We live on what we find — the earth is good to us. We can cook up a hedgehog as sweet as a chicken, and find ways to teach stingy farmers charity by wooing their dogs to silence as we slip into the henhouse. For everything the farmer has, he's taken from Mother Nature — and she is our mother too, who'd have all her children share her bounty."

"That's my belief as well," I said, "for I sometimes extract such a tithe from the rich men of the town. I'm sure it does them good in heaven."

He showed me some fine horses, a race apart from the poor swaybacked jades who carried their goods and babies. They'd been purchased at a horse-fair in the West Country, and were to be sold at the next market they came to, "if fear of the sickness hasn't driven the buyers away".

When the meal was ready, the women heaped my trencher with a rich stew of herbs and mushrooms and the flesh of the bird I'd seen meet its fate. One of them whispered in my ear, "After you've eaten your fill I'll take you to meet Aunty. She's been asking for you."

SHE took me to a drab tent that stood a little apart from the main encampment. Two young women tended a small fire just outside the poor-looking shelter. It was little more than a mound of mud-coloured sacking, but its guardians greeted me with grace and gravity. They lifted the flap of dirty sailcloth that served as a door, and ushered me into an interior blazing with bright colours, glowing in the light of a dozen candles, rich hangings, Turkey carpets, fringed shawls of scarlet and purple and green, all fragrant with spices. In the centre, cross-legged on a golden cushion, sat the oldest woman I'd ever set eyes on, whose bright black eyes glittered in a face gnarled like the shell of a walnut. I wondered if I should bow, or how I should salute her, for sailcloth and sacking notwithstanding, this was surely the court of the gypsy queen.

"Come and sit here beside me where the light's good," she commanded. "You're as strange a sight to me as I am to you. So let's have a good, long gape at each other, and then we'll talk."

She put two fingers in her mouth, and gave a piercing whistle, whereupon one of the women outside came in with two cups and a stone bottle.

"Blackberry brandy," she said. "My favourite tipple. You can drink it all night long and still find your head's clear as a bell in the morning." She poured me a brimming cup full. "Now tell me where you've been all week. According to the cards you were due last Monday. I wondered what was keeping you."

I sat there tongue-tied.

"You've been in the cards for a fortnight; you were in my own horoscope last week and everybody else's since Sunday, and you were definitely in the apple-peelings on Monday morning."

I shivered.

She tipped me a wink. "Frightened?"

"Your tent's chilly," I explained.

"Now take a sip of that brandy, which will warm you nicely — and believe me, the nectar of the gods isn't a patch on it. It will loosen your tongue, and a good thing too, for you're not the sort of fruit that grows on every tree, and there are many questions I want to ask you. You don't strike me as the shy and silent type, so I'll allow you a moment to find your tongue, because I'm an old, old woman now — one hundred and two on my last birthday — and my patience isn't what it used to be. My old granny used to tell me that senility brings tranquillity, but she was either a fool or a liar."

So we talked, or rather, I talked, for most of the night, telling her my whole life's history, remembering things I thought I'd forgotten. She'd nod and laugh and interrupt with questions. Sometimes my own answers surprised me, for they seemed to tell me things that were as new to me as they were to her. When finally I stopped talking, from sheer weariness, I found we'd emptied three bottles of brandy between us, and that the sun was rising.

"I'm afraid I've wearied you," I said, "keeping you awake with all my prattle."

"Don't be silly," she snapped. "When you get to my age you'll find you need little sleep, for you know there's an endless supply of it coming to you in the near future. Now go away and sleep — my great-granddaughters have made up a bed for you in their tent. Wander around the camp as you like, and bathe in the river, then come back and eat with me and we'll talk more. We're on the move again the day after tomorrow, and you might as well travel with us for a time. I'm sure there are things we can teach you, and — young though you are — I imagine there is a trick or two you might teach us."

"I know I can learn a lot from you, but what could I possibly teach you in return?"

"You're wise in the ways of the city," she said. "And ever since we've come to England, which was back before even I was born, we've always kept to the country and steered clear of the large towns. But I fear the world is changing, and we must find new skills. That's what the Romany have always done to survive."

THUS began my sojourn with the Egyptians. I spent my days as they all did: moving camp, travelling, turning my hand to a multitude of different tasks. I learned to carve wooden trinkets and toys — which the gypsies wore around their waists to attract the curiosity of potential customers. I learned to forage for food in the fields and woods, to read palms and Tarot cards, and look after horses. They offered to teach me to cook their favourite dishes — hedgehog baked in clay, and other such delicates — but I declined, for I think that cookery in my hands would be less a homely art than a deadly weapon. Although they all kept themselves strictly to those tasks they deemed proper to their own sex, they let me pick and choose among men and women's work, and never demanded I hold to one or the other.

Sometimes I'd go with the men to trade horses at a fair, keeping my eyes peeled for that old bawd Appellina so I could tell her what I thought of her duplicity. But she must have taken her establishment in a different direction, for I never got wind of them. So I concentrated on studying horses, for the gypsies are as learned in horseflesh as are Cambridge scholars in philosophy, but twice as contentious when their opinions differ.

They were also skilled at mending things — pots,

tools, anything wrought of wood or metal — and brought many objects back to useful life that their owners had abandoned. Where others saw nothing but a midden-heap they saw a gold-mine, for what they found they fixed and sold at good prices.

I often travelled with the women of the tribe, who walked their own circuit round the country, stopping at cottages to sell their wares and tell fortunes. I marvelled at their skill in reading characters and guessing secrets.

I puzzled over their uncanny knowledge: they knew which woman had quarrelled with her husband; who pined for children; who had far too many and wanted no more; who was a thrifty housekeeper; who a slut (these last buying bright beads and ribbons while their more prudent sisters purchased needles and pins). The Egyptians explained to me that it had less to do with magic powers than with shrewd observation, and their quick exchange of news. For gypsies tend to travel where other gypsies have gone before, and if one overhears any local gossip or chance remarks, she passes her knowledge on to others. They showed me the secret symbols they scratched on doors and gateposts, marks so small they were barely visible, but which spelled out useful information to eyes that knew how to seek it: two wavy lines to say the housewife here wants a child; a circle enclosing a dot to signal quarrels about an inheritance; a cross to mark house-holds unfriendly to gypsies, and so forth.

At night, after a rich ragout of borrowed poultry, or a mess of fish that had been teased and tickled out of a stream, I'd visit the Aunty. She told me the history of her people, how they'd wandered from lands far beyond the Garden of Eden, never resting more than a few nights in any one place over a hundred lifetimes. She told me of her seven daughters and forty-nine granddaughters, and how she was the matriarch of all this tribe. Even the elders, the men who made the day-to-day decisions and meted out rewards and punishments, deferred to her in all things. She carried all the memories of what her people had learned in their travels, and made sure this inheritance was safely bestowed among her daughters, for she expected to die within the year.

She taught me tricks to gull the credulous, who wanted only to learn if they'd live long, grow rich or marry well, and ways to read the future when it truly mattered — by the symbols of the Tarot, or the patterns descried in the flight of birds.

We spoke of love and lust in all its shapes and colours, and she laughed with me at my old folly of wanting to be a man.

She was avid for tales of the city — the intrigues, the struggles, the tricks of my trade — and soon seemed to know my friends and enemies as well as if she'd met them herself. I made her a present of a pipe and some tobacco, and told her she would be — as far as I knew — the third woman in England to smoke the weed, after myself and my old landlady Mother Bunch. She said she and the women of her tribe had smoked magic herbs since time began, although she confessed the tobacco-weed a novelty.

One night when I came calling she announced, "No blackberry brandy for you tonight. Try some of this instead."

She offered me a handful of dried-out mushrooms. "Strange fare," I said. "Talking to you is thirsty work, good lady. I think if it's all the same to you I'd rather have the brandy."

"It isn't all the same to me," she replied. "Try some and you'll soon think otherwise."

To encourage me, she took a handful of the dusty-looking morsels and chewed them slowly, as if savouring the richest suckets.

"You city folk are a timorous lot," she teased.

I'd not be outdone in bravery by anyone, least of all someone as old as my grandmother's grandmother, so I took a fistful of the mushrooms and gobbled them up.

"Now we'll sit quietly for a while and say nothing," she murmured. "Just listen to the sounds of the night — the music around the campfire, the rushing stream, the leaves rustling, the birds sleeping in their nests, the caterpillars turning into butterflies, the fish dreaming, the stars singing . . ."

And then I fell into a strange sort of waking sleep, listening to the old woman, who went on speaking although her lips never moved, seeing not only her face as she spoke, but the pictures that were in her thoughts. And I was with her people, travelling in many unknown countries of deserts and giants and pyramids and unicorns. The Aunty taught me how to fly in the air, and we held hands and her long grey hair spread out like a pair of wings and carried us aloft to an eagle's nest on the highest peak of a towering mountain. And then she set me gently down to earth on a rope made of cobwebs, and what should I see when I dropped to the ground but you, Bridget, fighting against a crowd of goblins, whose faces were hidden behind masks in the shape of wolves' and snakes' heads. So I came and fought beside you with a stout staff that once belonged to Maid Marian, and a silver sword that was made by the witch Morgan, and together we turned away the foe, who grew smaller and smaller until they were a crowd of mice and insects scrabbling in the dust, who all devoured each other. Then I was alone in the forest, where all the trees had eyes that stared at me, and you'd disappeared and I followed the sound of an owl hooting, until I realised it was my own voice crying out for need of you, and I was back in the tent of the gypsy queen, who was holding my head to her bosom as I wept.

"I think it is time for me to go away," I said.

"I know. Tomorrow we'll put you on the right road, and you'll soon be with her."

MOLL squeezed my hand. "And that's how I've come to you."

*Moll Cutpurse*

"Fly agaric." My aunt, who'd been listening avidly, spoke from her seat in the chimney corner. "It never varies. Powerful stuff, and sometimes instructive, but a dangerous game if taken too often. Still, I think I'd like your ancient Aunty, Moll. I hope you'll like Bridget's. Snuff the candles out when you're ready, children, I'm off to bed."

We sat, silently, until she'd retired to the far end of the room and closed the curtains of her box-bed behind her.

"I sleep in the loft," I said. "You might as well come too."

We climbed the ladder. I turned to face her.

"I suppose you think I ought to be pleased to see you — even after the way you abused me in London."

"And you," she replied, "now know what it feels like to be tracked down in your own private haunts and taken by surprise."

"As full of yourself as ever!" I scowled.

We spent the rest of that night forgiving each other.

FOR the next few days Moll and I wandered the countryside, gathering the herbs and flowers my aunt required for her pomanders and summer wine. Aunt Mary, very tactful, withdrew to her kitchen to boil up the rich fruits of the season into jams and preserves of brilliant reds and purples.

"They'd never believe this in Mother Bunch's alehouse," said Moll, staggering under a heap of marigolds, with rose petals tangled in her hair. "I feel like the bloody queen of the May."

"And how much will you pay me not to tell them?" I challenged. "There must be a few of your purse-cutting comrades who would never let you live down those flowers in your hair."

"Going in for blackmail, are we? I thought you too honest a citizen, my lady apothecary, to stoop to the cozening tricks of foists and coneycatchers. Why cut a purse when you can cheat on a customer? Why counterfeit coins when you can sell pills made of flour-paste? Why break into a house to steal the plate when you can be invited therein to physick the family with fraudulent remedies? Why receive stolen goods when you can poison for a price?"

I stuck out my foot and tripped her up. She fell flat on her face in the grass and before she could rise I was down on top of her.

"Still rankling over the elixir we sold you?" I enquired.

"Don't mock me, or I'll go back and join the gypsies."

"And all the gypsy queen will do is send you back again to me."

"Just what kind of power do you think you have over me? I'm bigger than you, and stronger as well. I think you've bewitched me."

"Well, love-potions are part of my stock-in-trade."

"If your famous elixir was anything to go by, your love potions wouldn't stir a tree in a strong breeze."

"Don't you malign me, you petty thief."

"You're as slippery a trickster in your own way as I am in mine, Mistress Apothecary. And I like you for it."

After all these years, it still seems passing strange to me that sometimes love comes first, and liking after. But there's no joy so great it doesn't leave you time to look out for the thunderbolt that may blast it all to pieces.

When we returned, and found my aunt standing ashen-faced in her doorway, I knew the bolt had landed.

THE farmer?" I asked my aunt. "What now?"

"Two of his cows are dead."

"Nothing for you to mourn about," laughed Moll, never the most sensitive of souls. "Your enemy's distress should be your delight."

"He says I've done it."

"You!" she laughed. "There's a pretty thought. Slipping out in your nightgown with a noose and an axe. Or standing on a ladder to reach up and slit their gizzards!"

"Moll," I tugged her arm. "I don't think you understand."

"Understand what?"

"He thinks I've cursed the dead," my aunt explained to her. "He says I'm a witch."

"He's called you a witch before now," I said, "and your neighbours would have none of it."

"He's found the parcel of herbs I gave his wife. He says I've not only cursed his beasts, but I've plotted to murder his unborn child."

"No one believes you're a witch."

"These are evil times — of death and disease and a foreign king that some say is half mad come to rule over us. You can feel the fear any time you walk abroad. When people are frightened, they'll believe whoever shouts loudest. And I fear this time he's bested me."

"What of his wife? She'll defend you."

"He's locked her up in the house. Says it's to protect her from the evil spirits I've set upon her."

"How did you get news of this?" I asked.

"After he shut her in he rode away. So she screamed until her nearest neighbour, old Mistress Curtis, heard her and spoke to her through a chink in the wall. She bade her come and tell me that her husband had ridden away for the magistrate. Then she fainted dead away. Mistress Curtis says that from the way she spoke, it sounds as if he's knocked some of her teeth out. I fear for her life if she's been beaten, for she's not a strong woman, Bridget, as you well know."

"Before you worry for her life," cried Moll, "worry about your own! If the constables are riding out to arrest you we have no time to lose. We must take you away."

"There's no use," sighed my aunt. "Mistress Curtis knows not how long she lay there, for he must have locked her up and ridden away in the small hours of the morning. If Mistress Curtis hadn't come to her door to return a borrowed paper of pins, the poor woman might be shouting still."

"A good three hours. For Mistress Curtis is a fat old soul, who walks with a stick, and it took her near an hour to hobble here from the farm. Ever since then I've done nothing but sit and stare into the fire, waiting for you to return, so I could warn you to get away."

"For *us* to get away?" I cried. "Not without you, Aunt."

"Where can I steal a horse?" Moll demanded. "There's no time to be lost."

"You must go without me," said my aunt firmly, "for if you carry me with you there's no doubt they'll hunt you down and charge you as my confederates. There is no place we could hide that would be safe from these hounds of Hell. But if you leave now, before I am taken, then you are nothing more than my niece and her companion up from London, who have paid their visit and are heading innocently home again."

"We're not leaving," Moll replied. "And they're not taking you. How much time do you think we have before they come?"

"An hour at most," said my aunt. "But heed me, and go quickly!"

"No!" roared Moll. "Forgive me, Madam, but you will heed *me* — and quickly. Now ask me no questions, and do as I say, and we'll have you and ourselves safe out of this by morning."

Moll turned to me. "I'll be back as soon as I can.

Meanwhile, make ready these things — an old sheet, some berries crushed fine, a few coals from the hearth, well-ground to a powder, and a paste of flour and water mixed. The other necessaries I'll find when I return. Let nobody in, even if you have to push the dresser and table and all against the door to bar their way — and whatever else, don't panic."

We quickly gathered up the necessaries Moll had so mysteriously demanded. Then I brewed us a decoction of camomile flowers, to soothe our spirits and strengthen us for the dangers ahead. We sat for a while before the fire, and I marvelled that my aunt seemed so calm, when I was rattling and chittering with fear.

"I've been expecting this," she confessed.

"I'd like to kill that man," I cried. "I'd hang him up by his heels and let the crows come and peck him to death."

"It isn't only his work, you know."

"But who else? Your other neighbours love you."

"Love me, maybe, but fear me, just a little, for my healing skills. And in a time of fear, one terror breeds another. Witch hunts, like plague, come round again in seasons. Sometimes they arrive together. We've been free of the infection here for many years, so now the fever bursts forth in a new visitation."

"Has it happened here before?"

"Every few years, somewhere in the neighbour-hood, there's a rumour that some old woman has poisoned a well, or that a younger one has stolen her neighbour's husband by charms and potions. Tales of women dancing naked with the devil on moonless nights. Sometimes the panic mounts, and a hapless woman must play the scapegoat. A witch's trial's a great diversion. It takes people's minds off their own troubles, to watch a screaming old woman trussed up and thrown in the pond. If she drowns she's innocent. If she floats she's a witch. If the stream won't have her, she must be the devil's own.

"My great-aunt — that's your great-grand-mother's sister — was proven innocent thus when I was a child. They apologised to her family for the false accusation, and gave her a fine funeral by way of compensation. I had a new lace cap for it.

"Or they can do what they did to poor Sarah Browne in the next village — and strip her without a thought for her age or her shame to seek the mark of the devil's kiss upon her privities.

"Then there's the ranting and raving of her supposed victims — the jealous neighbour lying to settle an old score, the child bribed by his parents to fall into fraudulent fits, the covetous farmer, like mine own true enemy, whose crops fail by his own negligence and whose beasts fall ill through his own mean feeding, who compels his family to counterfeit strange sicknesses, and produces hellish tokens he claims were hidden in his byre.

"Among the wild Scots I've heard tell they burn their witches as a public entertainment. So I'll thank my stars that the rope's a gentler fate, and a quick end to the mortifications that will come before it."

I tried, in vain, to cheer her, promising that such gloomy forebodings would never come to pass.

"I've seen enough of such things," she said, "to know that once this fever seizes a place there's no stopping it until the ghastly pageant has run its course."

There came a pounding at the door and my heart stopped until I heard Moll's welcome bellow: "God damn it, open up!"

She rushed in, seized me, and pushed me out the door.

"Don't ask questions. No time. There's a horse hitched to a wagon behind the house. Give him an apple to keep him quiet. And stay outside. You must listen for the magistrate's men. When you hear their horses coming, cough as loud as you can. Then stand before the door as they come up to you, and keep them talking until I open the door behind you, whereupon you stand aside and let them in."

I carried an apron full of apples round to the back of the house, where I found a sturdy cart-horse hitched to a wagon. I wondered how Moll had persuaded its owner to part with it, or if she had decided, as was her wont, that the horse, as one of Mother Nature's creatures, belonged to nobody but itself, and all she had to do was ask its permission and lead it away. And if it chose to bring a wagon with it, that was nobody's business but its own.

But my laughter at Moll's logic died on my lips, for I heard men and horses approaching. I crammed an apple between the horse's teeth, then ran to the front of the cottage and signalled Moll. I stood by the door and watched them come up to me.

The farmer, struggling to hide his exultation behind a pious smirk, nodded to the four riders, and they dismounted.

"Stand aside, young woman," said one, "for we are here on the King's business and must have words with your aunt."

"Of course, sir," I said, with an effort at becoming and maidenly courtesy, "but pray tell me your business, that I may advise my aunt of your arrival."

"The young whore knows what it's about!" cried the farmer, dancing up and down with impatience or an over-full bladder. "Move aside, she-devil, and let us pass!"

The door opened behind me, and I stepped aside. They pushed past me, as if afraid my aunt would fly over their heads on a broomstick before they could apprehend her. But no sooner had they entered the room than they stopped short, turned tail, climbed their mounts, and fled — for there in her box-bed lay my aunt, her eyes glittering feverishly and her face all disfigured with the red and purple tokens of the plague.

LATER that night, a cart-horse pulled a creaking wagon through the village, carrying my aunt's body wrapped in a shroud. I walked before the cart, leading the horse by the reins. Moll followed, intoning the doleful chant, "Bring out your dead! Bring out your dead!" We felt, rather than saw, the eyes at the windows, and heard the banging of shutters as each household locked itself away from the infection.

We led the wagon past the church and paused at the far side of the churchyard. I leaped on to the cart and Moll did likewise, taking the reins and setting the horse bolting along the track.

"Let's get out of here!" she cried. "Which way shall I go?"

My aunt, shaking herself free of her winding sheet, pointed east.

"That way," she said. "It's the last direction they'd expect us to head in. The London road's the other way."

"Not a bad old horse, this," shouted Moll as the wagon rattled along. "I knew when I saw her eyeballs she'd do better for speed than you'd guess from her bulk. The gypsies taught me many tricks for sizing up horseflesh."

"Keep your mind on the road," my aunt told her sharply, "or you'll have us in the ditch."

"A miracle recovery!" I observed, as my aunt wiped the plague-coloured paste off her face with a corner of her shroud.

"An old trick the devil taught me," said my aunt.

ᕼOWEVER shaken my aunt was by her narrow escape, and however unhappy at leaving her life-long home with no hope of return, she carried herself bravely. Rather than die in the place she loved, she chose to leave it, for she loved life better. And Moll spoke of a friend with an aged sister, down in Kent, who would welcome a companion in her rustic solitude.

"You'd be safe enough there, Madam," Moll reassured her, "for your persecutors here would never follow you to London, much less to the country south of it. I know these rural boobies — like fish out of water once they lose sight of their own church steeple."

My aunt coughed, but said nothing.

After an easy day's travelling, we reached the fishing port of Great Yarmouth. We'd decided among ourselves that we'd sooner risk plague in the city than witch-hunters in the fens, and we resolved to make our way to London by water.

"How will we get a ship?" my aunt protested. "We left in such haste I've nothing with me to sell or barter for our passage."

Moll smiled and chided her gently. "Leave such matters to me, Mistress Mary. For though you may be older in years, I am older and wiser in the arts of penniless travel."

We drove the wagon to the harbour, where the sea bristled like the spines of the porpentine with the masts of fishing smacks and coasters — for Yarmouth is the source whence the fishmongers of Billingsgate procure their prized red herrings, and indeed, if I had not know this already, the smell of the place would have told me so.

"Rest here," Moll commanded, "where you can watch the fishing-boats unload their catch, and by the time the last herring is packed off to the salting pans I'll have discovered all the news from London and booked our passage home."

"If any boats are landing there in plague time," I reminded her.

My aunt's weariness soon defeated her, and she fell asleep in the wagon. I contented myself watching the business of the harbour and wondering, with some trepidation, what changes we'd find on our return to London.

In half an hour Moll was back, triumphant.

"I've found us a boat," she announced in so loud and cheerful a bellow that my aunt woke and leapt out of the wagon as if the last trump had sounded.

"There's a foreign captain who leaves for London on the next tide. He'll take the three of us for a modest fee."

"A small fee's as bad as a large one," lamented my aunt, "for we haven't a penny between us."

"I've found the money and paid it," answered Moll.

"But how?" my aunt enquired, uneasily, I thought.

"Better not to ask, Aunt," I whispered.

"And what's more," said Moll, "if we fulfil certain conditions the captain will return the half of it at the end of our voyage."

It was my turn to be uneasy. "What conditions?"

"Well, he said he was in a hurry to get to London, for ill winds in the North Sea and some trouble in the Dutch ports delayed him sorely, and he's lost the chance of full five good cargoes. He vows that if he can't get to London and away again before the new moon, he'd as well drop anchor and roll up his sails forever. For time, he fervently believes, is money, and these weeks past he's lost more than enough of both."

"I am sorry for him," I said, "but what have these troubles of his to do with us?"

"As I said, he wants to get to London fast. He thinks he can do so if he has a good wind in his sails today. So I told him we'd raise one."

"What?" my aunt and I shrieked as one.

"Raise him one," repeated Moll, impatiently. "Conjure up a wind. That's why he took us on so readily. I told him we were witches."

We laughed to the point of tears, until I said, "What folly! He might have us arrested."

"Not bloody likely," said Moll, "for I took careful note of the cargo as his sailors carried it aboard. And it was clear to me, despite his clever ploys of conceal-ment, that there's more in that hold than a few hundredweight of herring. He knows if he tells anyone about us I'll denounce him as a smuggler. Or, what's worse, bewitch him and turn him into a toad. I'm not sure which he fears the most."

"How on earth are we supposed to raise a wind?" I demanded.

"I'm sure your aunty will think of something," said Moll with a sly grin. "And anyway, I only promised we'd try. Now hurry up and follow me, for our captain's impatient to catch the tide."

"What about the horse and cart?" asked my aunt.

"I've sold them to a gypsy," cried Moll. "Here he comes now to claim them.

And sure enough, a brown-skinned man with a scarlet kerchief at his neck approached. He greeted us most courteously, handed Moll a bag of coins, and led the horse and cart away.

"But they weren't ours to sell," ventured my aunt.

"Oh, did I not tell you? How forgetful," Moll grinned. "They were borrowed from your friend the farmer. I would have asked his leave before I took them, but he was away from home, hunting witches."

THE captain installed us in his own cabin, and regaled us with a fine bottle of wine, that had somehow escaped any tax or duty. The captain had his friends at the harbour here, and in exchange for a purse full of gold and a bottle or two of fine ruby nectar, the presence of many more such bottles in his hold had been conveniently overlooked.

Of course, when he put in to London, he'd have nothing but a cargo of smoked and salted fish for Billingsgate, and once this fragrant merchandise had been lifted away, not even the most zealous tax-collector would care to enquire too closely into the dark corners of the oily hold.

"Now, ladies," he said in his stilted English, after

some courteous conversation and a few sailor's tales of the wonders he'd seen, "I'll leave you to your preparations."

"Leave all to us, sir," beamed Moll as he departed, "and we'll raise you a breeze would blow you back to Holland." Then, when we heard him on deck, shouting orders to his crew, she turned to us and said, "Now, my satanic sisters, how shall we find a wind?"

"Don't be a fool, Moll," I replied, vexed at her pretensions.

"It isn't impossible," she protested. "What about those Scotch witches, who raised a storm against the Queen's coming from Denmark?"

"And were burnt for it," I reminded her. "And anyway, I doubt it's anything but a false tale to frighten children."

My aunt meanwhile sat humming to herself, rolling the wax that dripped from the candles into a soft ball, the size of an apple. She stroked and patted and pinched it all round, until it was the shape of some beast's head, with curving horns. She pressed some breadcrumbs from the table into the creature's chin and some hairs snapped from her own head to form a wisp of beard like a goat's. Then, carrying the little head, she motioned us to follow her, and ascended to the deck, humming an eerie tune.

She swept majestically past the Captain, scarce seeing him, for she appeared to be in a trance, and he stood with his sailors, all dumbfounded. She raised the horned head aloft and, with a terrible shriek, threw the image into the black water, raised her face to heaven, and began to chant in some weird, unearthly tongue. Her eyes glittering with the witchlight in them, she spat thrice into the water and lowered her head as if in prayer. The whole company stood silent for full quarter of an hour, until finally there came a sound like a giant, otherworldly bird flapping its enormous wings. We looked up to see the great sails, formerly limp and slack, begin to swell and billow with a fine fresh wind.

Bowing graciously to the captain, she led us back to our snug retiring-room below.

"How?" I asked, when finally I could find my tongue.

Moll said nothing, but looked at my aunt with new respect.

My aunt's eyes sparkled, with witchlight or wickedness. "I couldn't fail," she confessed. "I knew the blow was coming. In an instant or an hour I couldn't have told you, but come it would."

"I knew you were a woman of prodigious knowledge, aunt," I said. "But it seems you have some skills I knew nothing of."

"Perhaps," my aunt said sadly, "if there had been more time, there were many things I could have taught you."

"Do you mean," Moll burst out, "that the evil farmer's accusations were not mere idle slander? Come, you can confess to me, Mistress Mary, for I am far outside the law myself and will surely someday dance my life away at the end of a rope."

"There is an ancient wisdom," my aunt said solemnly, "and there are secret books."

"What books are these?" I asked, holding my breath.

"Pray tell us, and you secret's safe," begged Moll.

"My books are the clouds and the sky and the air and the water. If you silly city-born simpletons can't tell by looking about you when a wind is coming, then I know not why you think yourselves so clever. And we'll hear no more of your rude remarks about rustic coneys and country bumpkins, Moll!"

"The biter bit!" I laughed. Poor Moll looked chastened.

And so we came to London, light-headed on smuggled wine, the coins refunded from our passage jingling in our pockets, and smelling powerfully of good red Yarmouth herrings.

THE infection, so they told us at the dock-side, had abated, and only a dozen or so new deaths were counted these three weeks past. So we hastened first to my father's shop, for my aunt and I were eager to make sure of his well-being. Moll hung back, fearing that after her last encounter with my father she was forever persona non grata, but I pleaded with her to come along. When she readily complied I knew she understood my foreboding. And it proved, alas, that my fears were justified, for we found the shop empty and looted. A flock of kindly neighbours rapidly descended on us, vying to welcome me home with the news that my father was dead of the plague.

"He was a saint, your father," sighed the woman who had so often brought us pies instead of pence for her medicines. "He asked no money for his services to the plague-stricken, and did what he could for all the ailing souls in the neighbourhood. There's a dozen or more alive and well today in this street who would be bones in the plague pit now were it not for his ministering."

"Not like some," said another. "There were false plague doctors, with beaked masks stuffed full of herbs against the infection, who haunted the houses like great carrion crows, selling false hopes at high prices."

My own feelings about my father were so mixed, halfway between Moll's deep suspicion of him and my aunt's warm and sisterly devotion, that I only wept a little.

We sent my aunt off in the care of the woman who used to pay us in pies, and entered the shop. After my father's death, thieves had looted it, leaving only scattered papers and empty chests. All his drugs and powders were gone, and his books vanished as well. Shards of broken glass covered the floor, the sad remains of those he'd hoped would one day bring forth the Philosopher's Stone. There wasn't a candle in the place.

"Welcome home," Moll said ruefully.

"Why did we come back?" I asked.

"So your aunt wouldn't be hanged for a witch, so your livelihood wouldn't be gone forever, and so I wouldn't forget myself for the sake of a few blissful hours rolling with you in the sweet grass. London is home. Our lives are here."

"Changed days, alas. Half the people I know will be dead."

"Half the people *I* know would be better off that way," countered Moll.

"I want to open my shop again," I said. "My father, rest his soul, played so little part in the day-to-day trade of late — being far too busy with his alchemical mysteries — that I'm sure I can manage without him. But I'm sore vexed about the missing stock, for it's a tedious business assembling the necessaries. When I think of that treasure-trove of roots and herbs we left behind us in the country! There's not a sprig of pennyroyal nor a pinch of belladonna left here, and no money to purchase a new supply."

"Leave this to me," said Moll. "I'll see you set up in business again before the week is out."

"And how do you think you'll manage that?"

"That's for me to think on. Now go down the lane and comfort your poor aunt. Tell her I've gone to see a friend, to arrange her new lodgings in Kent. I'll come back and collect you both in two hours' time."

I found my aunt, sorrowful but much comforted, sitting at my neighbour's fireside. The pair of them were exchanging eulogies upon my father's virtues, making me wonder what stranger they were speaking of.

When I told my aunt Moll had promised to secure her a new home in the country she was delighted, for in the city she felt herself a fish out of water, and now that my father was dead and buried she had little wish to linger here.

My neighbour told me of the changes in the neighbourhood — the deaths, the looting, the unprecedented prosperity of those who had, shrewdly, contrived to profit by the plague, buying up abandoned property cheaply, asking extortionate prices for food and fuel, playing on fear.

She spoke of those friends who'd died; the family in the lane who'd been wiped out, the candlemakers across the way who'd sold their shop and removed to the country, the young bride in the next street who'd died within an hour of her wedding. There were some new faces in the neighbourhood, most notably one black-clad man-of-business named Brown, who'd come along in the wake of the death cart, buying up houses and shops from stunned widows and grieving orphans, and now owned fully half the buildings in our street.

"He wanted yours as well, my dear, but we told him you were away on a visit in the country, and would by no means drive an easy bargain when you returned. So you can expect him to call on you with an offer. If it isn't impertinent," she added, "tell me, what are you going to do with the shop?"

"Begin again," I replied. "Business as usual, as soon as I can manage."

"If only you'd find a husband to keep you," she sighed, "you'd find things so much easier."

My aunt bestirred herself from her mournful reverie long enough to suppress a snort of laughter.

Soon there came a violent battering at the door, which sent my poor neighbour frantic lest it were a debt collector or at least an invading army, but, as I suspected, it was only Moll, back from her errand.

"It's all arranged," she announced. "Bridget, you and your aunt will leave tomorrow at dawn. Mother Bunch is driving a wagon down to Kent to collect a load of hops for her beer. She'll carry you to her sister's village. She intends to visit her for a day or two, and that will give you time to see your Aunt Mary made comfortably at home. You might even find some herbs for the shop. You'll easily be home again by Sunday."

I drew her aside. "Mother Bunch! Is *that* your friend who has a sister in Kent? I'd never trust my gentle aunt to that foul-smelling harridan!"

"Hush," said Moll. "You misjudge old Mother Bunch. She may not smell as sweet as the morning dew and she may have seen the inside of the Bridewell more than once in her younger days, but she's a kindly soul, and I promise she and your aunt will find a thing or two in common before their journey's ended. After all, they're both in the business of making folk feel better — your aunt with her herbs and potions, and Mother Bunch with her half-penny rotgut. And they both have the same good strong shoulders from all the poor souls who've leant on them to weep out their troubles. And as for Mother Bunch's sister, there's more than one colour of kitten in a litter. She's a country woman born and bred, who puts me very much in mind of your own Aunt Mary. I know her well, for I've lodged with her myself, when once I found it needful to leave London in a hurry. Mother Bunch hid me in a barrel and sent me down to Kent in a wagon. I was sore cramped when we arrived, and reeling drunk from the fumes inside my hiding place, but a few days under the good woman's apple trees and I was all the better for it, not least because of escaping the gallows."

"And pray what escapade was that?" I asked, feeling there was more to Moll than I would ever fathom.

"Why don't you ask Mother Bunch?" she replied. "I'm sure the tale will while away some weary hours on your journey, if she cares to tell it. Now bring Mistress Mary along to Mother Bunch's, for she's preparing a room for her, and has promised me a fine fire. I'm sure your aunt could use a good night's sleep."

As we walked through the dark streets to Chick Lane, I trembled to think of my fastidious aunt's reaction to filthy old Mother Bunch, and thought of the contrast between her own sweet-smelling cottage and the foetid rooms above the alehouse. But my aunt, when we carried her there, was so overcome with weariness, and so grateful for Mother Bunch's aid, that she scarce noticed the crowded tavern full of sots as we

passed through it, and fell instantly asleep in a chamber
that surprised me by its cleanliness.

"Do you recognise this place?" grinned Moll.

I realised it was the same chamber we'd quarrelled in, the Great Hall of Moll's college for young pickpockets.

"She says it's easier to keep the place clean since I've been gone," Moll admitted sheepishly.

WE set off early the next morning, after a sound sleep undisturbed by the wild revelries and riots in the alehouse below. I found Mother Bunch's conduct to me much changed from the day she'd served as the surly Cerberus guarding the gates of Moll's little Hell. She recognised me now as Moll's friend, and her manner was warm and confiding. To my relief she'd even managed to clean herself up for the visit to her sister's, and she and Aunt Mary passed the journey chattering comfortably and sharing the reins while I clung on for sweet life in the back of the bone-rattling cart. I watched, bemused, as London receded once again before my eyes, scarce eighteen hours after I'd returned to her.

It was an easy day's journey to the village where Mother Bunch's sister lived, which pleased me, for I knew it would be possible to visit my aunt without difficulty. I was further delighted by the discovery that Mother Bunch's sister was no mirror-image of the slatternly tavern-keeper, but as sweet and cleanly an old body as my aunt herself, and overjoyed to have a companion to share her garden.

We stayed two days in Kent, while Mother Bunch negotiated a purchase of cheap hops from a farmer, and I saw my aunt happily settled in, arguing enthusiastically with her new house-mate over the efficacy of rotten apples as a poultice for rheumaticks, and admiring the excellent bees housed in four fine hives.

When we left, Mother Bunch's sister pressed on us an unexpected gift, a little pup from her mastiff's latest litter. We tucked it in among the hops, along with some herbs for my shop and a basket of fine, fresh eggs — "for that ruffian Moll, who will never eat them when she ought to".

Our journey home was slower, for the wagon was heavy-laden with hops just slightly rotten, that Mother Bunch said would do well enough for her hoggish clients. She was pleased at the good bargain she'd made, and, in an amiable mood, whiled away the time by telling me how she'd first met Moll.

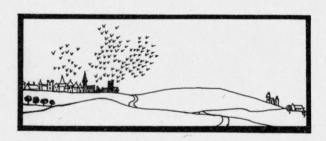

*Mother Bunch's Tale*

MY alehouse has sometimes been the resort of the poorer sort of players — not those who sing for their suppers in gentlemen's houses, but those who batter each other with tin swords to delight the groundlings, and trip each other up to reveal the hairy shanks under their ragged tunics — clowns and jugglers and mountebanks who are suffered in the playhouses to keep order in the pit before the poetical declamations of their betters.

Sometimes they come carousing with a great crowd of their admirers, who bear them hither from the playhouse with cries of "A drink for the greatest of all clowns!" "Wet the juggler's whistle!" Which favours they return with "More ale for this wise judge of the comic arts!" "Aqua vitae for this paragon of a spectator!" And so fervent are the toasts to each other's wit and talent, and so fast the swilling down of ale and cheap wines, that they are soon tangled in a snorting, drunken heap, with only the hardiest among them still raising his head to cry, "A toast to Harlequin!"

One day, after the playhouse emptied, the whole ragged crew came tumbling in, bearing aloft a boy on their shoulders — at least I thought it a boy — who shouted to the assembled multitude: "A treasure trove of gold! Drink up, my friends, for Dame Fortune has smiled and the drinks are on me!"

The youth waved about a great swollen pouch, wrought of gilded leather, that rang and rattled with a heavy load of coins. The strings of the purse were cleanly severed, as if by the blade of a swift and secret knife. The young cutpurse, for so he surely was by the sly, triumphant smirk with which he displayed his booty, tossed a shower of coins across the bar. I was hard-pressed to gather them before my guests pre-empted me. They were gold indeed — I bit them to make sure — but like no coins I recognised.

"A strange harvest," I told the young pickpurse. "I'm not sure your money is good."

"Gold's gold, isn't it?" he retorted. "The genuine

article. Can you say the same for the cat's piss you sell
as beer?"

I went for him, to box his ears, and that's when I
saw he was not man but woman. "Genuine article
indeed," I muttered, looking this curious creature up
and down.

"I'll take your money," I said. "But I'll have to
charge you extra for the trouble it will take me to
dispose of it."

"Fair enough," the cutpurse said. "There's plenty
here." She thrust the pouch under my nose. It was a
curious contrivance of many folds and pockets.

"What's that?" I asked, pulling out a paper that was
caught in a slit of the silken lining.

She snatched it away from me and scrutinised it.
"Gibberish," she announced.

The paper passed from hand to hand. There were
few among the company who knew their letters, and it
was turned every which way by greasy fingers.

"Greek, that is!" cried a player. "Who reads
Greek?"

"Give it here!" Tom, the red-haired poet, stood up,
dislodging the young apprentice he'd been fondling
upon his knee. "My brains aren't so addled as to make
me forget the Greek my tutors pounded into me."

He studied the paper, then shook his head. "Oh,
Moll!" he cried, suddenly sober. "Oh, Moll, my
thieving little androgyne, you have hooked a rare fish
this time!"

"What does it say? Read it out," she demanded.

"To do so might be treason," he whispered. "And I
rather like my head secure upon my body. These are
matters of state."

Fair enough that the rabble should be kept in

ignorance, but this was my alehouse and I felt it was my right to know. So I poured out the ale that Moll had demanded, to satisfy her companions, then withdrew with Tom and the cutpurse into my private chamber.

"Now read it!" Moll and I commanded him as one.

" 'My lords,' it says, 'the journey by sea and land was not without its dangers, but these are past now and I am safely arrived at the place appointed. Herewith the names and present movements of all the ships in the Spanish fleet, as promised in our discourse of September last. I trust this intelligence will be partial recompense for your boundless generosity in graciously allowing me shelter in your land. For though Spain may be my mother she has cast me out, and like a foundling I lie now in England's bosom, and pray I may drink here the milk of true Christian kindness, and spurn forever the withered dugs of the whore of Rome, that gives not milk but venom. With all greetings to your mighty selves, I await the messenger known to us both, who will carry this missive to your worships at the time appointed. Sending my most humble obeisance to your wise and gracious Virgin Queen, I remain your devoted and trembling suppliant, Luis Gomez de Gonzalez Vargas y Santo Domingo.

" 'On the reverse side behold the list of ship names and movements as promised. L.G. de G.V. y S.D.' "

Moll whistled. Tom shook his head.

"Oh, Moll," he cried, "where found you this prize? Not dangling from an unguarded belt at the playhouse, to be sure?"

"Well," said the cutpurse defiantly, "I'd rather not say."

"This is important, child!" he shouted, shaking her

— although she was near as tall as he was. "For those who steal state papers are traitors, and this is indeed some correspondence for the Queen's own ministers. Do you know what they *do* to traitors? Hanging's far too easy a death. They'll hang you up, to be sure, but pull you down again while there's still life in you, and slit you up the belly to pull your innards out and throw them into a roaring fire before your very eyes."

"Don't be a fool," I prodded her. "Tell us where you found them."

"Well," she said, "I was climbing along some roof-tops. Just for the sport of it, and to see what I could find in the way of unlatched attic windows. As I was moving along the ledge of a great stone-built house, my eye was caught by something inside an unshuttered chamber." She paused.

"What thing was that?" Tom pressed her.

She blushed.

"Come now, no coyness! This is a matter of life and death — *your* life and death. What did you see?"

"A woman undressing."

Tom suppressed a grin. Even I, who thought nothing could surprise me at my time of life, nearly burst out laughing.

"Well, she was beautiful. The fairest, smoothest skin I've ever seen, golden hair like a day full of sunshine. Like a goddess. Or at the very least a duchess. Then she picked up her mirror, and I think she must have caught sight of me, for she turned suddenly towards the window and I, fearful of being caught, tried to leap to another ledge. But I missed my footing, and would have been done for had I not caught hold of a balustrade as I slid downwards. I managed to hoist myself on to a broad ledge. There was a small window leading into a chamber; I tried it and found it unlocked. So, reckless as I am, I opened it. There was a man, fast asleep, on the bed. He looked like a foreigner, with beard and hair black as the devil. In a heap on the floor lay the most splendid suit of clothes I've ever seen. Rich silk and velvet, slashed sleeves, a lace collar that would make any noble lady with golden hair sit up and take notice. Temptation conquered me. So I bundled the lot into a velvet cloak that lay nearby, and departed through the window, climbing more carefully than before, back up to the rooftops, which I know as well as any streets in the city. Then I carried my booty safely home. It was only when I unwrapped the bundle at my own lodgings that I saw I'd lifted a purse as well. So I clipped it off, just as I would have done if its owner had been wearing it, and bore it to the playhouse, where I pretended to my companions that I'd cut it on the spot. I thought I'd keep the clothes a secret until the right moment came to surprise the world with my gallant attire."

"Oh, Moll," said Tom, "of all the sins and vices, vanity is the last I would have charged you with. But it seems that none of us is free of it."

"What about the paper," I interrupted, before the poet could launch forth upon a favourite moral discourse. "It's a dangerous business."

"No one knows I have it," protested Moll.

"Except all your boozing-mates in my alehouse. And there's not a set of tongues in England that can wag as they do. No, I'm afraid your secret is out."

"We must think on a stratagem to save her silly neck," said the poet.

"How long ago did you steal it?" I asked her.

"Perhaps three hours past, not more than four."

"Then there is just a chance," I said, "that the deed can be undone. Your weary traveller may still be asleep, or even if he's raised the alarm, there is one thing we can do."

"What?" asked the cutpurse.

"Return the property."

"But how?"

"The way you took it."

"What if they see me?"

"We'll aid your escape," Tom promised. "Mother Bunch and I will be waiting in the lane with a horse and cart."

"We will?" I asked, but the poet tipped me a wink, and I knew, as always with Tom, I was conquered.

Moll looked doubtful.

"Hanging's only the beginning of a traitor's death," I reminded her, "and they say the executioner operates upon his patients with an exceedingly blunt knife."

"I'll do it," she said.

I counted out the foreign coins she'd given me, and, reluctantly, replaced them in the purse.

$\mathcal{S}$OON after, Tom and I sat waiting in a wagon, in a lane behind a row of noble houses, fearful lest some servant enquire our business there, or, worse, appear round the corner leading a miserable Moll as prisoner. But to our relief, after scarce half an hour, we heard the pounding footsteps that could only belong to Moll.

"Done it!" she announced. "I know these roofs and chimney pots like the back of my own hand. I climbed from one ledge to the next, crawled along the balustrade, and slipped into the room with cloak and clothing and purse and all. And, lo and behold, there was the renegade Spaniard still fast asleep in his bed."

"So you escaped undetected."

"Well, not quite. When I dropped the goods on the floor of the chamber, the noise roused him, and he sat up. I told him that I was the scourge of all thieves and the Nemesis of all pickpurses, and was returning to him some property of his that a nipping rogue had tried to purloin. I declared that I would expect no reward nor thanks for him as I hoped to receive my recompense in heaven. Then I bowed and backed out of the room the way I had come."

"Did he say anything?"

"He merely gaped and goggled, rubbing his eyes as if I were a ghost or a visitation from the Night Mare. It was only as a climbed down from the roof of the stable in yonder mews that it occurred to me he might not speak our language, and may not have understood a word I'd said to him."

"We'll take no chances," I told her. "We're carrying you out of London. Climb into the cart and crouch down inside that empty beer barrel. And don't come out until you're bid."

Her bones must have been well rattled by the time we reached Chick Lane, but I thought the young fool deserved it for the trouble she was giving us. "Now, Tom here will take you to my sister down in Kent. Tell her I said to keep you for a month, and I'll square the cost of your feeding when I see her at Whitsun. By the time you return to London I hope and pray your Spanish friend will have forgotten your face, or at least have other matters to occupy his attention."

"What if I don't want to go to Kent?" she asked defiantly.

"Then the only safe course of action is to disguise

yourself. Perhaps you should paint your face and put on the attire more appropriate to our sex."

"I'd rather rusticate."

"Then get you gone."

"Still," she sighed, "it's a pity about those fine velvet breeches."

"Get down in that barrel," I thundered, "and don't show your ugly face until Tom's carried you safe across the river and well into Kent!"

QVINQVEFOLIVM

*Moll Cutpurse*  BY the time Mother Bunch finished her tale we were nearly home. I hoped that Moll had not taken it into her head to scale any rooftops in my absence. Not for fear of her losing her footing, or finding any more foreign spies, but — I am ashamed to say — for fear of golden-haired maidens in attic chambers.

Mother Bunch stopped the wagon in front of the shop, where Moll stood in the doorway, puffing her pipe.

"I have a surprise for you," we said to each other, in perfect unison.

"Mine first!" cried Moll, sweeping us into the shop. I stood in the doorway, staring round about me. I could scarce believe it. Where I'd left a bare and looted ruin, there now stood a tidy, well-stocked shop — its shelves bearing ranks of jars and bottles, its drawers and boxes full, as revealed by a hasty inspection, of the vital elixirs and powders without which no apothecary can ply our trade. There were scales and measures, mortars, pestles, retorts in all necessary sizes. On a shelf in the corner stood half a dozen thick books bound in brass and leather, and were it not for the total absence of dust on their covers, I would say they were the twins of those volumes that had been the very cornerstone of my father's library.

"Moll," I cried, embracing her, "you're a wonder!"

"It was easy enough," she said, "with you out of the way. I only hope I've put the right things in the right places. I'd be sorry if some poor wretch came in asking for a potion to plug up their bowels, and you, all unwitting, gave them something that would do the opposite."

"It all seems in good order," I told her, peering into the jars, sniffing liquids, tasting grains of powder on the tip of my tongue. "But how did you know what I'd need?"

"I went to Bucklersbury, where there are more apothecary shops than there are mackerels at Billingsgate. I studied their wares carefully, and asked a few questions of the shopkeepers. So I memorised a list of necessaries and set about obtaining them."

"Where from?" I asked, with the faintest tremor of suspicion.

"From a shop," she replied. "But now let me help you bring in your bundles. Mother Bunch will be wanting to carry home her hops."

"The bundles can wait," I said.

"And so can Mother Bunch," affirmed the tavern-keeper, "who is glad to be out of that wagon after a long ride. And I'm as eager as Bridget to learn how you came by this stock."

"What sort of price did you pay in Bucklersbury? That's a street of sharp dealers. Neither my father nor I would trade there if we could come by our supplies otherwise. We'll have to charge a pretty price to cover your outgoings.'

"There were no outgoings," said Moll, her eyes darting everywhere to avoid meeting mine.

My fears were justified. "You mean you stole the stock?"

"Yes, but . . ." she began.

I cut her short. "But nothing! Moll, how could you? I may put up with your ploys and delight in your cunning, and betimes shelter you from some punishment you probably deserve — but I will not ply my own trade with stolen goods."

"You'll change your tune," shrugged Moll.

"I'm sorry to be ungrateful. You've made a brave effort, and I love you for it." I tried to embrace her, but she shook me off. "Please don't be angry, Moll, but I have my scruples."

"You! Seller of false philtres and cures for hopeless cases. Scruples indeed!"

"Well, what of our own safety, then? If the owner of these goods finds us out, we'll be off to dance on Tyburn tree."

"The owner of the goods knows where they are," Moll said cryptically. "Why don't you consult those weighty tomes in the corner and see if the wise ancients have an answer?"

I opened the volume nearest at hand and discovered my father's name inscribed on the flyleaf.

"Our Herbal! Our Pliny . . . our Agrippa!" Each book in the collection, minus its familiar coating of dust, was as I remembered it.

"And the chemical powders, my most scrupulous lady, are yours as well — a little worse for wear, perhaps, some things having spilled or otherwise diminished in their travels — but it's the stock of your own shop, as near enough as I could reassemble it."

"Then were was it when it wasn't here?" asked Mother Bunch.

"In Bucklersbury. In the newest apothecary shop in the row. Presided over by a grey-faced, black-clad gentleman named Salathiel Brown. Dear brother of the selfsame man-of-business Eliphalet Brown, who has so perspicaciously cozened plague-widows out of their property, and orphans out of their birthright in this very street."

"And how did you discover this?"

Moll sat upon the shop-board and told us how it happened.

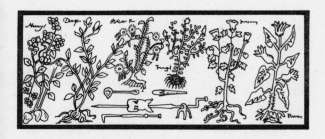

THE old laundress across the way told me what she knew of the looting. It was no ordinary thief taking his chances, but a calculated plot by Goodman Brown. He kept a careful watch on the house after your father was buried, and after some weeks had passed with no sign of your return, he and his brother came in a wagon and broke the seal upon the door. They carried everything out of the shop, bar a few glass vessels and papers which they broke and scattered upon the floor, to make it appear that thieves had entered.

The washerwoman was wakened in the night by the noise of the removal. She ran out, with a shawl thrown about her nightsmock, and was about to raise a cry for the watch when Brown himself emerged from the shop, bold as you please, waving a roll of paper all festooned with seals and ribbons, which he told her was a warrant for the salvage of plague-victims' goods if they died without living heirs. She protested that you were alive and well, away in the country. He countered that there was no proof of this; indeed, your absence from your father's death-bed suggested you were like as not dead yourself of the pestilence. He said his salvage came in the nick of time, for thieves had broken into the shop. She looked askance at this, so he pulled her inside and showed her the mess on the floor. He claimed his mission was for the public good — had she not heard of the apothecary's shop in the Strand, where thieves knocked over a vessel of volatile oils and caused a fire that killed twenty people in their beds?

When I went to Bucklersbury, that Jerusalem of all herbalists and apothecaries, to seek the necessaries for your shop, I heard the traders there complaining of a new man named Brown who'd opened up at the end of the row. He was underselling them all, and they doubted his credentials as a master of their craft.

So I went into his shop, and asked in all innocence if he were kin to another Brown, a pious man of property who dwelt near the Temple. Indeed he was, and even boasted to me of his brother's shrewdness, who had risen so rapidly to fortune. His sharp wits, the druggist said, were only exceeded by his piety, proving that God rewards his chosen few.

Then I walked abroad and sought out my young, scholars — such as had survived the plague — and enlisted their co-operation in an enterprise.

The next morning found a young girl, her face all blotched with a terrible rash, wailing outside Salathiel's shop.

"Camomile soap indeed!" she shrieked. "Poison more like! He's ruined my face! Spoilt my skin! What are my marriage prospects now?" she sobbed. "Pothecary Brown? No, Mutilator Brown, I say," and she wept as if her heart would break, unheeding the protests of Brown, who shouted from his doorway, "She lies! She lies! I never saw the wench before!"

An hour later, when the poor mottled child had finally wandered off, sobbing piteously, two beardless boys stationed themselves one on either side of the herbalist's door. One belched continuously, the other gave off a rhythmic volley of thundering farts. "Wind!" they cried. "Why such wind? Our mother dosed us this morning with a tonic from Brown's. A tonic for growing pains, he said. Well, it's taken our minds off growing pains for sure!" And they punctuated their laments with a great cannonade of wind from mouth and arse before beginning their tale of woe again.

The apothecary rushed out of his shop and made to kick them, but they tripped him up, and before he could recover himself, resumed their loud, windy plaints from a safer vantage point across the street, where an old lady sat roasting chestnuts on a brazier, chuckling toothlessly and urging them on.

The afternoon found a trio of mourning orphans weeping loudly for their poor dead parents outside Salathiel's door.

"They were hale and hearty yesterday," one sobbed. "Then they sent us to Brown's for spices to make mulled wine!"

"They mixed them in and heated the wine," wept the second.

"Then all at once they fell down dead," blubbered the third.

Salathiel Brown came out of his shop and cried that they were little liars, and made to drive them away with the end of his broom. But an angry crowd gathered, and murmured against his ill-treatment of such poor bereaved innocents, and began to belabour Brown with his own broomstick.

The crowd was peppered with my former pupils, and a pair of them, exhibiting the zeal of righteous citizens, came running with a pot of tar and a bag of feathers.

"He's a disgrace to the trade!" shouted a neighbouring shopkeeper, who had perhaps suffered more than others from his new-found competitor.

"Let's tar and feather him, then!" cried an old onion-seller, who wore his wares round his neck like a hero's garland.

Then, choosing my moment, I entered the fray, and rescued Salathiel from the angry mob. I pulled him back into his shop and bolted the door.

"I can get you out of this," I said, "for a price."

"What price?" he asked suspiciously, more fearful of losing a penny than of losing his life.

"The stock of your shop."

"The stock of my shop!" He was sore affronted.

"That's no great price, to be sure, for it isn't yours to sell. The rightful owner of these goods is back in London."

"Vile slander! The stock is mine!"

"I have witnesses who can prove otherwise."

"Produce them!" he challenged.

"I will, for the next court sessions. So prepare your forehead for the brand of thief, if the rabble out there don't get you first and fix their own penalty." Out the window we could see a trio of boys stirring the tar over the old chestnut vendor's fire. Another pair of boys came along with a great long log, preparing to batter down the door.

"At least the tar is good, sober Puritan black," I said, "but I fear a richly-feathered cope will smack of papistry."

"Get out!" he screeched.

So I did, and left him to the mercies of the mob.

The door fell in at the battering ram's second try, and I stepped aside as the crowd spilled into the shop. As per my orders to the young bravos who led them, no harm was done to the shop or its contents, save one bottle smashed by the kicking, thrashing feet of Salathiel himself as he was carried forth from his premises.

I did not linger to watch the stripping, the tarring, the rolling in feathers, but hastily whistled up two of my confederates to help me pack the stock and carry it out to a borrowed wagon. We had scarce begun the removal when we saw the unhappy apothecary ride off in state on a triumphal procession round the neighbourhood, mounted astride the stout log that had served to batter down his door. So well-coated was he with tar, so thickly masked with feathers, that his own dear brother would scarce have recognised him.

By nightfall everything was back in your shop and, by the morning, in what I hope is good order. The contents of his till I expropriated as a removal fee, although it was not as rich a harvest as I expected. It seems the pothecary Brown (if, indeed, he is pothecary at all) is not so sharp a businessman as his brother. Still, there was enough to send my young friends and helpers to a rich, greasy feast at Pie Corner.

So I hope this puts your scruples to rest, my love, for though I am no arithmetician I know that one theft plus another does this time equal no theft at all. For Salathiel can hardly charge us with stealing what was yours to being with.

*Moll Cutpurse*     "HIS brother," observed Mother Bunch when Moll's tale was told, "is unlikely now to prove the friendliest of neighbours."

"It seems he was no friend of mine to begin with," I replied, then kissed Moll mightily for full five minutes in partial recompense for her labours on my behalf.

But a sharp squealing from Mother Bunch's hand-

128

basket brought me back to the business at hand.

"My surprise to you," I said, "is scarcely so elaborate. It took me no effort in getting, but I hope it pleases you a little."

Then I opened the basket and lifted out the mastiff pup. Moll cried out with delight, then took the tiny creature in her hands, stroking and kissing it as it nuzzled against her. She crooned and whispered to it, and pressed it close against her cheek, rubbing her face against the soft new coat. Then she thrust the dog at me suddenly, as if it had bitten her, and burst into tears.

Mother Bunch and I stared at each other in an amazed and uneasy silence. I reached out awkwardly and put my arms around her, holding the pup in one arm, Moll in the other, the pair of them whimpering softly into my bosom.

When finally she came to herself, with a loud sniff and a vigorous wipe of her nose on her sleeve, she acted as if nothing had happened, and would give no explanation for her outburst. Instead, she gave Mother Bunch an account of all that had passed in her alehouse during our absence — it had been an ordinary week, with half-a-dozen brawls, a stabbing or two, but not one fatality, and the takings were better than average for the season.

"I've been as busy gathering news as I was setting up your shop," she said, "to find out who's dead of the sickness, who's profited by it, who's for marriage and who's for hanging in the months I've been away. Mercifully full half of my young pupils still flourish, and — alas — so do some of my enemies. But the saddest news is that poet Tom is gone, though whether it was the plague, the pox, or the drink that took him I know not."

Mother Bunch could shed no light on it, said he'd not

appeared in his usual corner one day and nevermore came to it. But in the worst weeks of the sickness she herself had closed up shop, and only lately had she resumed her trade and summoned back her faithful flock. This put her in mind of the hops that awaited her attention, so she took herself and her wagonload off to Chick Lane.

We settled the little mastiff in a basket beside the kitchen fire, and went early to bed ourselves, to compensate for the nights apart. Before we slept I asked Moll again about her tears over the pup.

"I brought her to you to make you smile, not make you weep," I said.

"She recalled to me a little dog I had once, these many years ago, when I was scarce more than a pup myself, of seven or eight. I loved the dog and cossetted it, and all the care that little girls are wont to give their dolls I lavished instead on that mastiff pup. For dolls always seemed to me naught but painted wood, while my dog gave me back as much love as I gave her. Yet one day a cruel, vicious boy who lived across the lane stole her away, and for a monstrous sport threw her into the river before my eyes. They say that dogs can swim from birth, but he tossed her so far that she soon tired of paddling and drowned before she came to the bank.

"Whereupon something burst inside me, and it was as if my blood all turned to fire, for I leaped upon him like one possessed, and bit and belaboured him in spite of his greater size and strength. I did not come away unscathed, for both my eyes were blacked, but he was the one who went bloodstained and blubbering home. My parents were puzzled that I should set such store on an ugly pup, for they said there were hundreds of finer ones in London. And if I were a good child, and learned to sew my seams straight, I should have another pup before the year was out. But somehow my seams were never sewn straight enough, and according to their lights I was never good enough, for their promise was forgotten."

"So now at last is your pup restored to you," I said.

"And a bitch, like her predecessor, so I'll call her by the same name."

"What was that?" I asked.

"Baby," said Moll, and was sore affronted when I burst out laughing.

T HUS we resumed our lives in London. Though Moll passed most nights with me, she kept her old chamber at Mother Bunch's, for I told her I would have no pickpockets' college in my kitchen. She herself felt it prudent to keep her more questionable friends and enterprises well away from my shop, "for there's guilt by association, and even though I might risk branding or hanging, I'll not have you suffer with me".

In time my shop began to prosper (for, in truth, the business flourished better under my sole charge than ever it did in the care of my father, who was more interested in discovering the elixir of eternal youth than in supplying Mistress Jones with a cure for her monthly cramp). I was sorely tempted to ask Moll to put aside her dangerous dealings, for in time I had money enough to keep us both. Yet the one time I even hinted at such an offer, she pounded her fist on the table and said she'd be beholden to no one for her living, not even those she loved. She stormed out of the house in a vile temper, Baby close at her heels, and I saw nothing of her for the rest of the week. Never again did I suggest it, for I know that had she offered to keep me in the same manner I would have been equally adamant in my refusal — and not because her earnings were so-called ill-gotten gains. For both of us, the knowledge we lived beholden to no one was more than half our fortunes.

We passed our days plying our separate trades, and spent our evenings apart as often as together. Sometimes Moll absented herself for days at a time, "to take a breath of sweet country air, and ride horses", or so she said. Indeed, she often came back smelling like a stable, but I knew that horse-riding was only half the story. For London rang with travellers' tales of a highwayman who was really a woman in disguise. I hoped against hope that this bold robber was not Moll, but one of the other so-called roaring girls (for as her fame grew, so did the number of those who sought to copy her). Still, there was nothing I could do, for I had long ago resolved to hold my peace and stop my ears. If I strove too hard to change my darling's ways, I would likely lose her altogether.

Those who knew us thought it strange that Moll and I lived so long together in such harmony, for we were as contrary as sun and moon in our tastes and temperaments. She loved crowds, noise and feasting; I preferred my books, my potions and my solitude. We shared a few friends in common — for I may be a scholar, but I'm no hermit — but mostly we lived as if in different countries. Yet this, I think, was all to the good, for when we came together we never tired of each other's company. Nor did this comfortable companionship ever dampen the fires of our lust for one another.

On Sundays, when the shop was shut and Moll in a mind to rest from her labours, we'd sometimes call on

friends in their houses, or drink with some well-chosen
companions in our favoured taverns. But Moll was
never one to mix her work and her pleasure — those
she dealt with in the line of her shadowy business she
allowed no part in her private life, save Mother Bunch.
She might sit down for a politic sip of ale with some
receiver of borrowed goods, or frequent a thieves'
boozing-ken for news of sharp tricks and rich pickings,
but when she supped with her friends she supped
elsewhere, and drank in taverns well away from the
haunts of her colleagues.

From her years spent sniffing wistfully round the
playhouses, Moll was a great friend to the actors. She
was surprised to discover I knew some of the players
better than she did — having cured their children's
colic, treated their wives' chilblains, and supplied the
purges whereby they did penance for too much
festivity. For unlike Moll I had no need to keep my
trade and my pleasures separate. Those I dealt with
often became my warmest friends.

The midwife of the neighbourhood: "Wormwood,
centaury and blessed thistle, please, for Mistress Pine's
queasy stomach; also a paper of fennel seeds to bring
poor Avis's milk on. Twins were the last things she
needed, poor child."

The whores would seek to forestall the midwife's
visit: "Could I have more of whatever you gave me
last time, please?"

The cook from a near-by great house came for her
cloves and cinnamon: "They've ordered more cakes
for tonight than ever they'll consume, all to make a
brave display for the new in-laws. Come tomorrow
for nuncheons, and I'll save you the broken meats."

The lady from an even greater house, who came in a

closed carriage from another part of the city: "I brought him a dowry of rich lands; he's given me a wedding gift of the Spanish pox."

We went often to the playhouses, up to the Fortune, or, in fine weather, crossing the river to the Globe. Moll had her drinking-mates and tobacco-brothers in both companies, and after their labours ended we'd sometimes carry off poets and players for a night of pipe-smoking and drunken disputation. Alas, Moll's generosity was such that my shop's stock of the odoriferous herb was frequently depleted. "Courtesy of the house," she'd announce magnanimously, producing a great handful of the stuff she'd spirited off unnoticed from under my counter. But I kept a tally of her borrowings, and had my own ways of rendering her a reckoning before the night was over.

On one such night, after a disaster-ridden performance of some blood-soaked tragedy (wherein the tiring-house wall collapsed onto the stage and half the players stumbled through the final scenes in a drunken stupor with their lines forgot), we found ourselves enmeshed in an argument, that grew more heated with each bottle of wine.

"They never existed!" asserted Will Sly, an actor, in a peevish temper because of the sorry performance. "Amazons are but a fancy like the centaurs, or that legendary race of men who wear their heads below their necks."

"But even the worthy Herodotus tells of them," I said. "And Sir John Mandeville, in his book of travels, tells of a visit to their country."

"Take all such stuff with a pinch of salt," advised Middleton, a play-maker who, in his cups, fancied himself a philosopher. "Even the immortal Homer, an indisputable authority on the means of building ships, the names of the Greek and Trojan commanders, the deployment of weaponry and many other historic matters, parts from truth when he sings of quarrelling gods and envious goddesses. Your Amazons are a dream of poesy."

I grew angry. "Then I suppose you'd have me throw all my books out of the window. Use Aristotle to kindle the fire and wrap up parcels with my Pliny. The ancients may not be holy writ, but there is much that a judicious reader can learn from them."

"You stray from the thread of the argument, Mistress Bridget," Middleton protested. "My quarrel is not with the old poets and philosophers, but with the notion of a race of women warriors, who made brave soldiers turn tail and put whole armies to flight."

"And why not," enquired Moll, leaning across the table and seizing the play-maker by the shabby collar. "I know nothing of these mouldering dead philosophers you and Bridget talk of, as if they were your own old playfellows and shared the same wet-nurse — but I know that I for one could better you in battle any day."

"But you, kind Moll, are a marvellous freak of nature . . ."

"I'll hear none of that!" she roared, shaking him until his teeth rattled and spilling everyone's wine. "There is nothing I can do that most of my sisters couldn't do if they put their minds to it. They're only as weak as they think they are . . ."

"And if they think thus," I put it, "it's because of the men who have convinced them of their weakness, that they may rule over them."

"But Nature . . ." protested Sly.

I cut him short. "Mother Nature is a woman too."

"Enough of this logic-chopping!" cried Moll, releasing Middleton so swiftly his head knocked against the wall.

"But is it not Mother Nature's way," interposed Will Sly, "that the man, more warlike, shall go forth and do battle, while the woman, of gentler humour and more feeble strength, shall serve him by keeping his house and bringing forth his babies."

"I defy you," said Moll, "to find me a man more willing for battle than I, and of as fierce a humour as my disputatious Bridget."

"Perhaps, Moll," ventured Sly, "you have not yet found the man to master you, and when you do you shall marry him."

In the same instant as I flung my wine in his face, Moll kicked the bench out from under him. He sat stock-still on the floor, gazing up at her in dumb surprise. Then, very gently, she picked him up, wiped his wet face with her kerchief as lovingly as any mother would wipe her babe's nose, and set him carefully back upon his seat.

"Why," she asked meditatively, "should I yield to any man, I who can make any man yield to me?"

"And why," I asked, "should any woman do likewise, whether her superior strength be of the body, the wit or the spirit?"

"It seems to me," Moll remarked, "that wives to their husbands are at worst slaves, at best whores."

"Why whores," asked the player, "when chaste wives cleave always to their one husband?"

"They merely rent out their private fields to be tilled and seeded on a longer hire," Moll replied, "and if they wish their fee — that is, their keep and their credit — they must yield up their obedience along with their bodies. All husbands, say I, are whoremasters."

"I fear you are unjust," protested Middleton, "for surely there are husbands who respect their wives as partners and honour them as helpmeets. Do these men not merit praise?"

"They merit only to be remarked upon as rarities," Moll replied. "And to praise them would but impress upon them that they are out of the common way. It would be as if you singled out and praised the dog that shitteth in the straw in the corner, which is what all dogs ought to do. What you must do instead is single out and beat the dog that befouls the turkey carpet, which should never be countenanced. But, alas, it is the bad dogs that are everywhere, and so the others are seen to be uncommon good dogs, instead of merely being dogs that do as they should."

"Your conceit escapes my wine-addled wits," confessed Sly. "But do you mean to say that you will never marry?"

Moll tipped me a wink. "Oh, I may well marry," she said. "When lack-land fathers seek not to buy their spendthrift sons estates and manors entailed in the body of a richer man's daughter. When men strive not to purchase themselves a faithful servant who asks no wage but a few words mumbled before a minister. When a woman can get her pleasure without paying for it with her life. When these things come to pass, on the seventh Sunday of that month, I'll let any man take me to wife."

"In truth," cried Middleton, "you are a poet, Moll. But I like not your philosophy, which bodes ill for all my sex."

"Then use your rhetorical art to put your brothers' houses in order," she counselled him. "Until then all you say is wind and empty disputation."

"This wrangling is thirsty work," cried Middleton. "Now who's for a drink?"

"Now you speak sense, good Middleton," beamed Moll. "Your folly is forgotten — though not forgiven."

But before we could summon the tavern-maid there was a commotion at the door. Baby, who'd been curled up asleep under Moll's seat, rose up and began to bark. The crowd of drinkers fell silent as a most outlandish figure strode into the room. He was well over six foot tall, and made even taller by the high cork heels of his scarlet boots. Yet he had no more flesh on him than a shadow, and resembled a tree branch in winter, that might snap in half at the first gust of wind. His hair was a bright and startling yellow, and so curious was his dress that it was no surprise when his broken speech declared him a foreigner.

"All attend me!" he shrieked. "I present myself. Johannes von Mecklenburg und Tübingen von Königsberg von Klops. Master Swordfighter. Duellist supreme. Champion of sixteen kingdoms. At your services. Arrived in Engel-landt today only just."

"Blown across the Channel by a fresh wind, from the look of him," Moll observed in a booming whisper.

"Silentz! I have come for the challenge."

"A sharp trickster," whispered Sly, delighted. "Watch him at work."

"Being greatest swordsman of Prussia I offer all Englishers a chance to test skill. For small price to defend honour of king and country. Big prize if you beat me."

"I'll take him on!" shouted a beetle-browed little man, who'd been sitting alone in a corner, scowling into his tankard.

"Go to!" cried Middleton. "You scarce come up past his belly, and you're drunk withal."

"I'll try my hand," insisted the little man. "Here's your fee, Dutchman! Now who's for a wager?"

"A shilling on the high German!" called the tavern-keeper, and the betting began — with only Will Sly putting money on the little drunkard.

"You're more of a fool than he is," Moll informed him.

"I know this game," Sly whispered. "Hold your peace."

There was one small difficulty. The challenger had no sword.

"For such happenstancings I come goodly equipped," proclaimed the German, producing an extra sword from a scabbard concealed within his many-coloured cape. "Small fee of farthing only for hire of instrument."

"I'll stake him," announced the tavern-keeper, tossing a coin to the foreigner. "Now push back these benches, good people, and I'll take your orders, please, before the duel begins."

In the far corner, well away from the rush to the beer-barrels and wine casks, the tall foreigner began a wondrous series of limbering-up exercises, great kicks and flexings, shouting "Hup! Hup! Hupla!" as he put himself through his paces. Across the room his challenger rendered himself fit according to his own lights, by swallowing a brimming jug of brandy, and wielding his borrowed sword as if it were a water-man's barge-pole.

"Positions, gentlemen," called the tavern-keeper, as he locked his money-box and bade his small boy sit upon it. The rest of us gathered round the space that had been cleared in the centre, with those at the back standing on benches and tables, to the great peril of their jugs and tankards. The German removed his cloak and handed it ceremoniously to the tavern-keeper, while his little opponent stripped off his doublet to reveal a stained and ragged shirt. The German struck a fine pose, with sword uplifted in a chivalrous salute. His opponent, with weaving steps, lifted the sword and struggled to remain upright.

"Begin!" cried the host, and with a clang of swords the duel was under way. In a flash of swirling metal, arms and legs the contest proceeded, and we saw to our amazement that the little drunkard, though seemingly an indifferent swordsman and tipsy with it, was more than a match for the arrogant foreigner.

"Gott in Himmel!" shrieked the German, "thou hast beaten me!" His spindly legs gave way under him, and he fell with a clatter onto the floor.

Amid cheers and laughter, even from those who'd lost their wagers, the little man acknowledged his victory.

"Now what about me prize," he demanded of the fallen German.

The foreigner tossed him a handful of silver. "It was a mistake. But there — I am no liar. Take it!" He staggered to his feet. The little man pocketed his winnings and strutted triumphantly out the door.

"And what about my winnings, host?" cried Sly.

"You've done well," said the tavern-keeper grudgingly.

"I know this game," said Sly, "so send us down

another bottle of wine — the best in the house — and keep what's left over."

Then, to everyone's surprise, the tall German once again commanded silence. "Now," he demanded. "Who's for another try?"

The offer was greeted with laughter on all sides.

"Should such a slight to the master-swordsman of the Palatinate unavenged go?" He was incensed. "Who dares doubt mine skill? A second try, for mine honour, gentles!"

Made bold by what they'd seen, half a dozen put down their coins — three actors from the Globe who thought their own swordsmanship on stage surpassed any skill found among the laity; an old soldier who fought in the Low Countries; two youths — vain upstart coxcombs — bursting to display the fruits of their fencing-lessons. Only the German, protesting loudly about mis-steps and sudden fits of giddiness, dared place a wager on his own behalf.

His challengers, smirking, settled among themselves the order of their going, for they all feared that the poor lunatick foreigner would be thoroughly vanquished and exhausted before they'd had their turn to triumph.

Then what a transformation we beheld, for as the first combatant, a player, approached, the foreign spindleshanks leaped into action and became in truth the mighty swordsman he'd first claimed to be, slashing the actor's shirt to ribbons with a few swift strokes as the cocky grin faded from his opponent's face.

"Try we for first blood, mine friend?" asked the German.

But the player cried quits, and the German gestured

141

towards his crowd of would-be challengers.

"Next?" he piped.

They fidgeted uneasily.

He smacked his sword against a table, making the tankards leap and the contestants tremble.

"Next is who?"

"Just a fluke that was," snarled the old soldier. "Just a fluke. I'm not afraid of a base-born foreign Dutchman. I know a trick or two. Make way!"

But the soldier too was roundly beaten, and stumbled away, cursing.

"A fine bit of gulling," whispered Will Sly. "The swordsman sends his partner ahead, who bides his time and feigns drunkenness. And when the crowd sees the seemingly foolish challenger triumph, they reckon they can do as well, not knowing the fight was a clever sham. It's a trick I've not seen these many years, ever since the French wrestler and his confederate walked off with twenty pounds from Bartholomew Fair."

"Nexxt!" hissed the high German.

But the other combatants had retired from the field.

"Perhaps then," he beamed at the onlookers, "I shall sell some of you a course of my fine fencing lessons, yes?"

"Ho, fencing-master!" It was Moll, leaping over the table and pushing her way through the crowd.

"Hsst, Moll." We tried to pull her back.

"Your swordsmanship is passable," pleaded Middleton. "But only passable. He'll slaughter you."

But Moll would not be dissuaded, even by my most menacing looks.

"I'll try a duel with you," she announced. "Here's your fee." She handed him a coin, which he slipped into the pigskin purse at his belt, swollen now with his night's winnings.

Then he caught sight of Moll's grinning face, and peered more closely at her. "Gott in Himmel! A vooman!"

The tavern crowd, who knew her well, cheered mightily. But the German stood horrified.

"Stand down, mein Fräulein, and take back your coin, for the master swordfighter Johannes von Mecklenburg und Tübingen von Königsberg von Klops shall never duel with the chentle sex."

"Gentle sex?" she repeated. "Gentle sex!"

"This swordsmanship is man's matter, meine kleine honeybee. Not for veak vimmen!"

"Weak!" she thundered. "Weak! If you don't stand your ground and fight me it is you who are the weakling, Master Prooshian Pisspot!" She appealed to the crowd, who cried their assent: "You show him, Moll! Give her a chance, Dutchman!"

"Is against all laws of shivalry," he bawled. "Myself I not so lower!"

"Coward!" she jeered.

"Coward? What coward? You dare to call the master fencer of all Prussia, the champion swordsman of the Palatinate, the duelling terror of Heidelberg, a coward? Leave duelling to your masters!"

"Masters?" she bellowed. "Masters!"

"Presumptuous vench! Get ye back to your cookpots and your distaff!"

"Distaff!" she roared. "Well, try *this* staff!" And swiftly she seized a stout broom from out of the hands of the gaping pot-boy, and began belabouring the German about the head and shoulders.

"On your guard, Dutchman! We'll fight with wooden swords this day to save your silly skin!"

He backed away, but she pursued him, savagely laying about his flailing limbs.

"Now take up your sword and fight, you braggart!"

But as he went for it Moll walloped him so well that he staggered, and she seized the moment to strike him a blow in his spindly shanks that tumbled him to the floor. In an instant she was down on top of him, pummelling his face and boxing his ears while he screamed and blubbered and shouted for mercy in a voice that suddenly savoured less of Germany than Yorkshire. The crowd of onlookers, fearing the racket would summon the watch, pulled her off him. He groped for his cloak and stumbled from the tavern, leaving a trail of the spots that dripped from his bloodied nose.

"Pardon me, comrades," said Moll to the assembled company with a maidenly blush, "for my ungentle behaviour that so ill fits my meek and timorous sex. But I hate a blatant fraud, and I'm sure you will forgive my lapse of courtesy as a well-meant effort to punish him for gulling you, and a means of censuring his calumnies against my sex." She produced from her doublet a pouch bursting with coins. "For here's the Dutchman's purse, made pregnant with your folly. I beg you, host, lay midwife and deliver it up as drink for all." She winked at me. "Now us honest folk must home to bed, for it's early to work in the morn." And she swept out, with the mastiff at her heels, and myself, Will Sly, and Middleton hard behind.

"Sweet Moll," said the play-maker, when he and Sly took their leave of us at Temple Bar, "I confess myself roundly beaten. Of ancient Amazons I can make no claim, but I'll stand surety we have one among us now."

I N the spring of the year I resolved to plant a new medicine garden, for the plot behind the house, wherein my father and I had raised many plants we needed in quantity, had long decayed. Despite her moans and protests Moll was pressed into labour. For all that she was strong as an ox she had her idle humours, and would sometimes sooner ride than walk, or, better still, lie abed and not go forth at all. So grouchingly she set to work beside me, turning over the earth and performing such labours as might coax forth a harvest from the soil. Our neighbours too were out in their several gardens, which adjoined each other in a maze of snickets, hedges and crumbling walls. Back to back with ours lay the garden of our beloved friend Mavis, who devotedly tended her fine trees that yielded fruit for jams and wine and puddings to last the whole year round. Mavis was a brave, strong-minded dame, well on in years, who'd seen her own fortunes rise and fall and rise again on Fortune's whirling wheel. She'd buried two husbands — the first a man of substance, whose lands were forfeited in Bloody Mary's reign, from which mishap he never recovered. He took first to drink and then to religion. She vowed it was the second that killed him, "for a minister's bands did fair constrict his bull-neck and saw him off in an apoplex. So he left me poverty-struck and pregnant, and went to take up his country curacy in Heaven."

Against the wishes of her friends, who urged her to bide her time for a better match, she next married a grimy-handed bricklayer, "a hard-working provider, God rest his soul, for myself and my orphaned babe. He was far too tired from his honest day's work to bother me unduly with his dusty embraces." She was devoted to her son, Ben. She'd early perceived his genius, and feared necessity would perforce bury his talents forever under his step-father's brick-heap. So she'd chivvied and scolded and bullied him to be ever restless and ambitious, and now he was a rising poet and playwright, with important friends at court.

"A passing good poet," said Moll, who knew him well, "but a pale shadow of his mother when it comes to spinning a tale." For our Mavis was the staple of news for all the neighbourhood, and not a kiss nor a quarrel in the parish escaped her notice. She sat not in judgment, as some lovers of gossip, but savoured the comedies and wept for the tragedies in the lives of the people around her; she relished every detail her numerous informants carried to her.

Sometimes, when we grew thirsty from our labours in the garden, she'd come to the wall with a tankard and we'd pause from our toil to drink of her ale and eat of her news. ("It would scarce be courteous to weed and hoe while the old dame talks," said Moll, in defence of an hour spent gossiping for every ten minutes of gardening.)

One day Mavis came to my shop, bursting with news. Her son Ben had paid her one of his customary visits, whereby he exchanged a great bundle of soiled linen for a neat pile of clean clothes and a hot dinner. She said he'd received a generous gratuity for devising the triumphal arch at Temple Bar, that was of late the King's stopping-place on his great procession through the City.

"So Ben gave me a great purse full of coins, and bade me buy some delicates and treat my friends to a feast in his name. He's a good boy, who loves his mother."

I smiled at this, for the good boy who loved his mother was a paunchy, bibulous scribe of thirty winters, marked out for me by his ill-concealed contempt for womankind. However, even such a doubting Thomas as I need not shiver outside the sunshine of Ben's benevolence, for I was bidden, along with Moll, as a guest to the banquet, "for there's a young friend of mine," cried Mavis, "I'd like the pair of you to meet."

Moll, when I told her of the invitation, graciously consented to forgo a profitable afternoon passing false coin at the Royal Exchange. We arrived at Mavis's door to find her receiving a great basket of sweet-meats from the pastrycook's boy. She carried us into her parlour, and presented us to her friend, Judith, who crouched on the floor, investigating the contents of a great chest of books.

"Some of Ben's," explained Mavis, "for his landlady said she was sore weary of dusting them all, and threatened to raise the rent in compensation for her extra labour. When he protested that her rapacity was a sore burden on a poor poet, she told him either they went or he did. So I'm giving them temporary shelter until he finds a more amenable dwelling-place."

Judith, wrapt in this printed treasure-trove, scarce acknowledged us beyond the barest greeting, and bent again to the books. I judged her to be only a few years older than I, but her face was a well-lined map of care and sorrow. When Mavis finally coaxed her away from the books and brought her to the table, to partake of a rich spread of tarts and tansies, she begged our pardon for her discourtesy, saying it was her life's dream to be left alone for a year in a chamber full of such books, if someone would only supply her sufficient food and fire. She spoke with a world-weariness that fitted ill with her rustic accents.

"Are you visiting from the country," I enquired, as Mavis bustled round the table, filling up our tankards with her potent home-brewed ale. "You don't sound like a Londoner."

"I'm fresh up from the country these ten years and more," she replied, "and sore regret it." She would say no more, and busied herself with ale and honey-cake.

Mavis, fearing that her little feast might languish in sobriety, filled the silence by exclaiming over her son's latest accomplishments.

We had, of late, been treated to a royal pageant, when the King and all his Court rode forth into the City, to be greeted at every turn with banners and declaiming poets and noble arches surmounted by allegorical statues. Mavis's precious Ben, she confessed, had been the architect of the day, the projector who planned it all, down to the drapery of every plaster goddess His Majesty cast eyes upon.

"It puzzles me," mused Judith, toying with the crumbs before her, "that the mere likeness of women, frozen into statues, should be permitted to figure forth emblems and allegories, queens and goddesses, whereas the living, breathing woman in the flesh is altogether barred from representing anything or anyone. And we must have men with piping voices aping us upon the stage."

"You should be fast friends with Moll," I told her,

who has lamented loud and long upon this very theme. Indeed she herself once ran away in disguise to be a player."

"I hadn't the wit or the aptitude for any disguising," Judith replied, "but I too ran away from home, carrying a sheaf of poetry I'd writ myself, that I hoped might buy my entrance into the players' company."

"She's of a talented family," Mavis explained. "Her brother's a celebrated playmaker, like my Ben."

"Don't speak of him in my presence!" Judith commanded. And, her tongue loosened by the good cheer at Mavis's table, she told us her story.

I DO NOT share the world's high opinion of my brother, for he sore betrayed me when I needed him most. He was some years older than I, and I was still a young maid when he fled to London. I was the sole defender of his honour, for he departed in disgrace. He'd got our neighbour with child, reluctantly wed her to save the babe from bastardy, and then neglected the both of them to bury himself in books and daydreams. Little wonder she was sore vexed, and grew shrewish, and less wonder that he was miserable, for I never saw a pair so ill-matched, and wondered at their coupling. Yet as rapidly as their patience with

*Judith's Tale*

each other diminished, their progeny increased.

I think she was secretly relieved one morning, when she arose to discover he'd slipped away in the night. And as long as he sent her money to maintain their babes, she was content. The rest of the neighbourhood was less quiescent, roundly condemning him for a laggard and a layabout. Only I spoke up to defend and praise him, saying his wit needed a broader stage than Stratford to strut upon.

My family was most displeased at my outspoken expression of such unpopular opinions, which waywardness they feared would dim my marriage prospects. This threat did not trouble me, for I never saw myself as a likely bride. In my childish folly I had aped my brother's bookishness, and painstakingly practised my letters by a stolen candle-end at nights. I wanted nothing more than to be a poet. Though I had little poetry to judge by, save my brother's scribblings and the precious copy of The Shepheardes Calender I filched from under his pillow, I felt my own efforts were as worthy as any other verse I'd seen.

My parents chided me: they said that maids must stitch up seams instead of sonnets, and lie in a man's bed instead of in his bookcase. But they were kind parents withal, and said if I comported myself modestly, and stopped singing my disgraceful bother's praises, and acted decently ashamed of him like the rest of the family, they'd find me a fine spouse. A gentleman, if I was lucky, who'd been up to Oxford, and perhaps even one who wrote a little verse to while away the time. Like that nice John Stroud, whose mother openly praised me in church on Sunday past. Old Stroud, John's father, was the richest wool-merchant in the county, and not over-long for this world, to judge by his colour.

Try as they would to make the match, I came up with one excuse after another, taxing my inventive wits as sorely as the writing of a five-act tragedy ever could:

I was too young. Nonsense, said Mother. When she was my age she was carrying her second baby.

I suffered the green sickness. Pity, said Mother, and dosed me with foul-tasting tonics.

I was in love with another. Excellent, said Father. Who is his family and how much does he stand to inherit?

I didn't want to marry, not John Stroud nor anyone else, now or ever. Brain-fever, said my father, and locked me in my chamber for a fortnight with no fare but bread and water.

John's mother came daily to enquire after my health, bringing a fine duck's egg or a gooseberry tart, which the rest of the household devoured on my behalf. John's father called on us every night, and carried my father off to the Swan, whence he came rolling home cursing and singing, shouting through the door that he'd break my arms, legs and neck in rapid succession if I didn't yield. John himself came only once, on the last night of the fortnight, and slipped a paper through the crack under the door. It was something he fondly imagined to be a sonnet, and, simpering at my parents, he took his leave. After I heard him depart, I snatched up the paper and read his clumsy rhymes. For the first time in my imprisonment, I laughed aloud, falling into such fits of shrieks and giggles that my bemused family feared I'd finally turned mad, and unlocked the door with an alacrity whose source I know not, after so long a spell of near-starvation. I burst forth out of the house and disappeared into the darkness. I heard my parents in pursuit, but they were fat and short-winded, and knew not the neighbouring woods and fields as I did. Hiding in breathless terror inside the hollow stump of an ancient tree, I heard my father shout, "Hell mend her. Let's go home. She'll come creeping back when the rain falls."

But for good or ill no rain fell that night, and I ran to the cottage of an old woman I knew, shunned by most folk because of her wall-eye and harelip, but a true friend of mine, and the only one I dared read my scribbles to. She said she'd miss me sorely, but she gave me bread and cheese and set me on the right road to London before the sun rose. I always carried my poems about me, concealed in a pocket I'd sewn into my petticoat, and with these I fondly hoped to earn my bread in London, which shows what a green girl I was.

Beware the kindness of the men you meet upon the road, for there was not one, on that long, long journey to London, who did not offer to be my protector, and not one who did but subject me to all the offences he'd offered to protect me from. I was in a sorry state indeed when at last I came to London, having torn my clothes, worn out my shoes, and lost my maidenhead along the way.

A young housewife in the liberties kindly gave me a bed to rest in, helped me mend my clothes, and washed away the worst of the mud and bloodstains. Then she pointed me in what she thought was the direction of the playhouse, though she said she'd never been there, for her husband and chickens and cow and babies kept her too busy for such idleness.

So I went in search of my brother, innocently

expecting him to welcome me with open arms and introduce me forthwith to all the playhouse managers, who would then read my works and commission me to write tragedies, histories and comedies. I found the ordinaries and taverns frequented by the players, and indeed my brother was well known in all these places. However, he did not appear to be in London, for the only news I could get of him, delivered with a leer, was that he was "away with my lord in the country". However, overhearing me receive this disappointing news in a pie-shop, a gaily-clad young man hastened to my side. He announced that he, Nick Parry, was a bosom companion of my brother's, and would consider it an honour to be my protector until my brother returned to the city. Now as you can well understand, I had by this time had my fill of protectors, but he assured me that he and my brother had sweated upon the same stage, even written comedies together; and, with a tear in his eye, he swore that I put him in mind of his own dear little sister, dead in childbed these two years past in distant Devon. He said further that, without undue modesty, he confessed to being one of the most promising players in the realm, and would no doubt have his own company to manage before the year was out.

Now remember that in spite of my recent sufferings I was still a foolish girl with hayseeds in my hair, consumed by the wild hope that I might live as a poet. By his warm and familiar talk of my brother, I came to trust Nick Parry a little. So I mentioned, somewhat shyly, that I carried with me a small sheaf of writings which I hoped might attract the interest of some important patron, for I scarce knew how such business was handled, having little understanding, besides my brother's hearsay, of the workings of the playhouses.

Nick seemed truly interested, vowed there was no reason he could see that a woman shouldn't be a play-maker, and bade me come home with him.

I hesitated, but he pressed me, saying his darling little wife would make me welcome, and this allayed my fears. So, stopping only at a vintner's to purchase some bottles of canary, which Nick said gladdened his wife's heart and satisfied the longings she suffered, being heavy with child, we walked through the city and out again. As we walked, he spoke of his own brilliant career as a player, but I scarce heard a word he said, so open-mouthed was I with true rustic awe at the wonders and horrors of London.

We came at last to a place I later knew as Islington, and he led me to a strange, tumbledown old house. I had never seen the like, and asked him was all this his, but he said it was formerly the mansion of some mouldered-away gentleman, and was now a common dwelling-house or tenement, wherein some two dozen folk had their several households, alone or in families.

Now we from the country are well-used to strong smells, for our cowsheds are never very far from our kitchens, nor our midden-heaps distant from our doors. But never in all my life had I smelled the foul odour of so much humanity compacted up so close together in a small and airless space, with so many different (but equally foul) dinners being cooked, so many overflowing chamber-pots, so much noise of screaming infants and their brawling elders.

He led me up many stairs and through winding passages, and bade me wait on a dark landing, outside a door riddled with worm-holes. He called in, "Oh, Sweetings, are you about? I've brought a guest. Oh,

Sugar-sucket, answer . . ." and disappeared within. In a few moments he emerged, disconsolate, waving a scrap of paper.

"Alas, she's left me this note (by the hand of a neighbour, poor Mouse, for she cannot spell a word to save her life) saying she's fallen ill and has gone to her mother's. Now I know she would never forgive me if I denied you our hospitality, and you must come in and bide here as our guest, putting up with such poor comforts as I can offer until my wife comes home and can entertain you properly."

If I'd my wits about me, I would have realised he no more had a wife than a pair of wings, but I was tired and frightened and sore vexed at my brother's absence from London. So I yielded to his importunities. That night, my will further weakened by wine-bibbing, I let him bed me. He exclaimed with delight when he found I was no virgin, for he said that taking my virtue would have weighed heavy on his conscience. Within a day or two the truth was clear to me that there was no wife, nor ever had been, but by that time things between us had progressed so far that I forgave him the lie and was willing to step into that imaginary creature's place. For her was a cunning charmer, who saw that the way to bend me to his will was not by frivolous compliments, but by the earnest and critical scrutiny of my writings.

He promised to introduce me to the important players and managers, but for many days we lived in a blind fog of excess — drunk on canary, dizzy with lust — and scarce left his chamber. I asked him why he didn't go to the playhouse, for even I knew that players had to labour many hours to memorise their words and gestures. He told me he had but recently concluded a brilliantly successful season, when he'd played a dozen parts to the wild acclaim of the populace. And now, in reward for his efforts, the company's manager had reluctantly granted him leave so he might rest.

I asked him if we could walk abroad and see a play, but he explained that if he but showed his face at the theatre, his admirers would mob him and pay no attention to the play at hand. And, though it made him blush to say it, there were many women among the audience, who, though he'd never spoken to them, had conceived a jealous passion for him. Were I to appear on his arm these envious jades would tear me limb from limb.

But these pretty excuses only stayed me for a few days, and I began to importune him until he grew angry. He called me a nagging slut; I said he was an idle braggart, and I would go and deliver up my works to the playhouse managers on my own behalf. He jeered and said these were great men who had no time to see silly country wenches. If I handed them a sheaf of poems they'd do naught but wipe their greasy fingers on them. I replied that I saw little alternative but to chance it, for he seemed loath to help me.

At which he broke down and wept, declaring through his tears that he loved me, that I was a true prodigy of a poet, a delicate plant that he sought only to cherish and nurture. Hadn't he read over my poems an hundred times, praising their virtues, and making judicious suggestions for the amendment of such few faults as he found. Any delay on his part had been but for the choosing of a propitious time, when the managers were like to be in sweetest temper. For they were impatient men, of a choleric humour, weighed down by cares. Knowing how to court their favour was all important. But if it pleased me he would beard the lion in his den, and take my work to the playhouse this very afternoon.

Soon we were both in tears, then so busy consoling each other that the day was ended, and we had gone nowhere.

But, good as his word, Nick went off the next day, bearing my precious papers. In humble gratitude I passed my solitary hours scrubbing and polishing the filthy, cramped room we dwelt in. He came in late, redolent of canary, still carrying my poems. Alas, the mighty Henslowe was abed with an ague; the great Ned Allen was closeted with a playwright these twelve hours, arguing over some amendments to a prologue. Burbage was nowhere to be found, but it was rumoured abroad that he was hiding from his creditors.

And so it went for a fortnight. Either we dallied at home — for if Nick had no other talents, he was indeed an ardent lover — or he walked abroad with my works in vain, coming back with an endless supply of plausible excuses. I asked him for news of my brother, but Nick said he still lingered with my lord in the country. When I enquired of Nick's plans for returning to the stage, he declared there were no plays in the present crop that suited his talents, and we could manage well enough for the present on his last season's earnings, thanks to my economical huswifery. Sometimes I sought to pursue my own writing, but for some reason the sight of me bent over my papers seemed to excite his lust, and all such efforts on my part led me nowhere but back to bed.

Finally, losing patience, I announced that I was weary of his empty promises, weary of fetching water from the pump to wash his wine-spotted shirt, weary of haggling at the cookshop for broken meats and burnt pies at half-price. I loved him well, and it broke my heart, but I was leaving him on the morrow, for I had to be true to my dream and become a poet, where now I was little better than his whore.

As was his wont, he first erupted in anger, then began to weep. He said it was the duty of all true poets to starve and suffer for their Muse. If I wanted a comfortable life, I'd best go back to Stratford and marry some rustic swain who'd keep me as fat and sleek as his sheep. Then he vowed he esteemed me more than any player ever did his wench, and if what I wanted was to be made an honest woman, why then he'd marry me himself.

I said I sought to be a poet and a playwright. Marriage, if it came at all, must follow after. He said I was a mistake of nature. I said he was a liar and a cheat, and I would leave him this very night.

But he snatched my poems from my hand and vowed he would deliver them straightaway to Mr Henslowe, or die trying. He bade me keep his supper warm for him (two cracked eggs I'd cadged at quarter-price from a hen-wife) and departed. Many hours later he returned, triumphant, declaring that the mighty Henslowe had received my papers with his own hand, and had promised to give them his attention. Although, Nick added, there was a pile of other papers higher than my head that stood awaiting his notice, and took precedence over mine.

So for many weeks I waited eagerly for news. Impatience made my temper short, or so said my protector, for we grew quarrelsome, and our battles became as heated as our coupling had been formerly.

Then one night Nick came home so drunk he could scarce undress himself. I sat him down on the bed and pulled his boots off. As I did so, I saw a hole in one boot, stopped up with some papers. To my horror, I recognised them as my own writings, all torn and muddied. I shook my drunken lover as hard as I could — what of Mr Henslowe? What said he of my works? Nick laughed and hiccupped and merrily confessed that he had never yet seen Henslowe at all. Gathering such surviving scraps of the papers as I could, I waited until dawn, crouched miserably beside my snoring lover, then departed.

I found my way back to the city, for in all my time with Parry I had never once left Islington. In the actors' haunts there was still no news of my brother's return, but in one of the ordinaries where I pursued my quest I found instead work as a serving-maid. The hours were long, and my only payment was my food (from such scraps as the clients left uneaten) and a pallet to sleep on beside the kitchen hearth. The work made me weary, and every night I was sick at my stomach. At first I imagined this was due to the rank steam and greasy vapours of the kitchen. But then I counted up the time since last I bled, and realised to my dismay that my unchastity had come to the usual conclusion. There was little I could do save stay where I was until my belly swelled.

One afternoon, as I carried a steaming basin of rabbit pudding from the kitchen, someone seized me from behind, turned me round, and struck my face a resounding blow. The assault sent the basin crashing to the floor, and splattered myself and those around me with a scalding flood of meat and gravy. Yet I scarcely noticed the cursing and commotion, for there before me stood my brother, purple with rage. Throwing the hostess a handful of coins "for your trouble, madam", he pulled me hurriedly from the eating-house and down the lane.

"What monstrous folly is this, Judith?"

No loving greetings, no exclamations over how the time since our parting had changed me (he, for his part, had lost much of his hair, acquiring in compensation a small pointed beard and a gold earring), no questions as to my reasons for coming to London. Only a torrent of hot abuse for the way I had dishonoured him. Reports had reached him of my search for him, my taking up with Nick Parry — "that bombastic jackanapes, that disgrace to the brotherhood of players. No manager would hire him again if he were the last player alive!" and — worst of all — my lunatic hope to be a playwright. For it seems my erstwhile lover had laughingly bruited my fantastical ambition about all the players' drinking-dens, making it a source of much merriment. Already the jest had gone round all the playhouses, that now I'd come to London to write plays, my illustrious brother had gone down to the country to sew and spin. He would not have me shame him so, and if he'd known my childish scrawls would have led to such madness, he would have torn up the first poem I'd ever writ.

I asked him why he thought the freedom he'd claimed for himself in leaving Stratford couldn't also belong to me. His only answer was to slap my face, pull my hair, and drag me off to find a carrier who would send me home in a wagon.

So broken-hearted was I, and so blinded with fury, that I forgot all my affection for him. I struggled free of his grasp and bolted down the nearest alleyway. In his high-heeled boots he was easily outdistanced. I hid until dark in a foul-smelling cellar, sick and sobbing.

In my desperation I thought, first of all, of returning to Nick Parry. But even if I swallowed my pride and forgot my anger, he would deny that the child was his — and, in truth, I could not be sure that it was, after my sufferings on the road to London.

I thought upon suicide. Whatever hellfire I might suffer for the murder of myself and my unborn babe seemed of little consequence compared to what I'd suffer if I went home in disgrace to Stratford. And the prospect of remaining in London, bathed in the white heat of my brother's scorn and my own humiliation, was equally intolerable. So I found my way to the river, for I knew that I had neither the weapon nor the courage to stab myself, and I dreaded poison's lengthy agonies.

As I wandered through dark lanes and alleyways, I prayed I might be set upon and murdered by some footpad, which would spare me the agony of cowardly indecision and leave my soul less tainted for later reckoning. Alas, no such lucky accident befell me, and soon I stood on the edge of a wharf, with a chorus of quarrelling voices murmuring into my ear: Jump in! Live! Die and be safe! Live and try to miscarry! Die! Live with your shame and be a mother to your bastard! Jump in and find rest! Go home and seek your parents' forgiveness! This last prospect was too terrible to contemplate, so I hurled myself into the river.

I was prepared for the cold, but the foul stench and taste of the water caused me at once to spit and retch and struggle. A waterman heard me thrashing about, and hauled me into his boat with a slippery pole. I doubt he believed my protestations, when once I'd stopped coughing and could speak, that I was no suicide, but had merely fallen into the river. Still, he asked no questions, merely wrapped me up in a great cloak that stank of dead fish, and carried me home to his wife. From what she said to him, I guessed I was not the first fish he'd caught that way.

The effects of my immersion brought on a violent chill, and she put me to bed. In the night I cast forth the scarce-formed life from my womb. My hostess expressed no surprise, nor disapproval, and tended me as expertly as any midwife. When in a few days she deemed me recovered enough to leave her house, I sought some way to repay her kindness. She said there was nothing; I pressed her. I had no money, but neither had I ties or obligations, and if there was any way my youth and my newly-recovered strength could be of service to her, I would be honoured.

She confessed that there was a favour I might render her. To supplement her husband's meagre earnings, she sold broadsheets and ballads in the Leadenhall and other markets round about. She bought them from the printers in great bundles, and eked out a few pennies' profit distributing them among the public who sought such novelties. But after purchasing a new stock, she had lately been sore troubled with rheumaticks, and could neither walk abroad nor cry her wares with the necessary vigour. Now two hundred ballad sheets lay in her press, and if they weren't sold by the end of this week, they'd be old wares and good for naught but wrapping fish.

I offered to go out and sell them for her, and despite her protests, carried them off, coming back at the day's end with a pocketful of coins and only half a dozen sheets unsold.

So between ourselves we formed a partnership, for she knew all the printers of such wares in Paul's Churchyard and Fleet Street, and had an eye for those songs and tales that would catch the liking of the crowd. And I, surprising myself, found I had a good strong voice to cry our merchandise and sing snatches of new ballads to tempt the customers. Our earnings were small to begin with, but as I learned the trade — and learned the ways of the city — I increased our profits. When my benefactress died, these four years past come Easter, she bequeathed me her share of our small but thriving enterprise. Now I walk no more abroad, but have my own small market stall, where I sell tales of great deeds in far countries; murders in the shires; the jests of Tarleton and Will Kemp; songs of love, betrayal, greed and death; tragical and comical ballads; moral tales; revelations of the dark doings of the Devil. My humble wares are a long cry from Sidney's noble *Arcadia*, or the richly-wrought verses of the *Faerie Queene*, but let those jeer who will, for I do what I set out to do — I earn my bread through poesy.

WE were, by this time, dizzy with the ale, which had flowed freely through Judith's telling. Moll, grown maudlin-drunk, blew her nose and vowed she'd make all her friends buy their ballads only from Judith, and woe betide anyone caught humming a song or repeating a jest that came from another source. Mavis carried in a great wheel of cheese sent up by "her cousin in the country", and as she passed round bread and butter the talk turned to more general matters — the differences between the old Queen and the new King, "coming down here with his rag-tag army of wild heathen Scots," complained Mavis, "who might as well be speaking Dutch for all I understand their gibberish."

"It's not the Scots that trouble me," said Judith, "for they're a race of fine storytellers and have carried down some new tales I've sold to my profit. But there's another army abroad in the land, whose numbers increase daily; these sobersided pious hypocrites who crawl like insects out of every corner of the city. These Puritans who would shut down the playhouses, drive songsters and ballad-sellers off the streets, forbid all games and dancing, dose us all with a dozen sermons a week, and command the stationers to print nothing but pious tracts . . ."

"Which, to give them their due, are a fine cure for sleeplessness," observed Mavis.

"Indeed!" Moll agreed. "They're a rising plague upon the city, who would ban all sport but church-going and all art but cheating one's fellows in the line of business. Even this parish is polluted with them, save the stews and thieves' kitchens, where their glum faces are never seen."

"Yet they will venture bravely anywhere there's money to be made," I said. "And I think if you look behind the bawdy-house keepers, and discover on whose behalf the pot-houses are run, you'll find that the wages of sin become translated by some alchemy into the spotless account books of such worthies as our virtuous neighbour Eliphalet Brown."

"Old Thunderface," cried Mavis. "I know him well — he holds the lease of half the houses in this street. His face is all pulled down at the mouth as if he suffered eternal stomach-ache."

"Let him come along to Bridget," Moll jeered, "and she'll sell him a purge he won't forget. They're enemies of long standing."

"*I* pity such a man's wife," said Judith, "for these glowering divines are so often petty tyrants in the bosom of their families. As they cross the threshold they turn from solemn patriarchs into screaming, colicky babes."

"For sure," said Mavis, "you need pity Goodman Brown's wife no longer, for she tired of his virtues and went off these two years past with the man who tends the Bear Garden on the Bankside. Pity instead his little daughters, for though their mother took them away with her, he filched them back again."

"I've often seen them in the street," I said. "Twin sisters, no more than eight years old. They never speak, and walk about with grave little faces. I offered them some cinnamon suckets once, and they ran away as if I were the devil's dam."

"The very ones," said Mavis. "Zeal-of-God and Discipline Brown."

"Alas, such names for the poor mites," said Moll, sniffing into her ale. "What a life they must lead. It makes me weep."

"I'm sure their father would be delighted if you

did," said Mavis, clearing away the broken meats of the feast.

IN the warm weather it was our neighbourhood's custom to pass much of its time out of doors. We cast open our windows, and carried out stools and benches to perform all possible labours in the welcome sunshine. Artisans hammered, housewives mended, and shopkeepers like myself set up our stalls in the street. I brought out a table, and covered it with jars of summer tonics, rose and lavender waters, and other goods befitting the season, and for once it seemed my trade was all of health instead of illness. On Sundays the street lived even more fully in the open air, passing our idle hours exchanging news of the neighbourhood, and debating upon matters of state and religion as if we were the Privy Council.

Ours was not a street of punctilious church-goers, but as if by unspoken consent this was never reported to the parish, so we were spared fines and other vexations. The only odd man out was the worthy Eliphalet Brown, who led his sombrely-clad babies out in solemn procession three times each Sunday to hear various preachers rattle out warnings of hellfire. So sanctimonious was he in fulfilling his religious duties that Moll feared he would have our whole street — women, children, men, dogs and all — hauled up before the bawdy-courts on charges of atheism and missing Sabbath service. But I pointed out that he too was guilty, for he avoided our parish church of St Bride's and deemed it a warren of popish superstition. He preferred instead to seek out the dusty corners where like-minded sectarians sang their clients to sleep with attacks on sin and bishops.

Moll herself in this fair weather was scarce to be seen at home, even on Sundays, going off with the ever-growing Baby, who was now the size of a small horse, on her shadowy business. This became, from time to time, a sore point between us, that we had so few idle hours together. But Moll maintained that in this season she must, like the farmer, take advantage of the weather, and be out in what she called her fields, taking in the harvest before chill winds and lean pickings came again.

On one such summer Sunday there came into our street a great noise of horn and drum and jingling bells. The children rushed in a great shouting flood to the street's turning, where two boys appeared, one tootling a horn, the other beating a great drum strapped round his middle. Behind them came a cloaked figure in a broad-rimmed hat, leading a great shambling brown bear on a rope. The bear's guardian tipped me a wink: it was Moll, incognito until Baby came loping after her.

"Who's for a dance?" she bellowed. "Who'll invite old Ursinus here to leap a lavolta? Who'll bid him dance a dumpe? Here's the finest beast in London of the bearish blood royal — nephew to the great Sackerson himself. He'll gallop for a groat! He'll caper for a farthing! Who's for a dance?"

Gleeful children stamped and pattered home to their parents to beg a coin. Even their elders, for whom no newfangled bear would ever be so brave as the noble old bears of their own youth, pressed forward for a look. The drummer-boy came round with his cap, and as soon as a few small coins glittered within it, the merry music started and the bear began his tricks. The music grew louder, in vain effort to match the shouts and cheers of the children. Soon most of the occupants of the street had crowded round, or climbed onto benches and window sills to see over the heads of their neighbours. From my vantage point, in my own doorway, I could scarce see the bear, but took my diversion instead in the faces in the crowd.

Farther down the street I heard the clatter of shutters flung open, and saw two little white-capped heads bob out of an upstairs window. It seemed the jangling music and merriment had even penetrated into the grave, Sabbath-keeping house of Eliphalet.

The bear's antics grew wilder and wilder, and the crowd roared its delight when the animal, with an agility belied by its bulk, turned a double somerset and stood on its head. But through our neighbours' laughter I heard, all of a sudden, a shrill, piping scream, as one of Eliphalet's daughters, leaning too far out of the window, tumbled down to the street below. At first only those on the edge of the crowd heard the noise, as the fallen child continued shrieking and her upstairs sister began to howl in concert. I ran to the little girl, whose hands and knees were cut and bleeding. She had reached out her arms to break her headlong fall, and from the way she lay I feared she had broken one of them. Fortunately, her father's house was as low and mean as its proprietor's frowning forehead, else the poor innocent might have been killed.

Her shrieks continued, which was a good sign in that she had not fainted away, as so often happens in a great fall. After a brief survey of her injuries, I deemed it safe enough to lift her from the dirt she lay in. I called up to her twin, still blubbering at the window, that she had best summon her father if he was at home;

this suggestion made her howl all the louder.

I thought that I could do more for the child if I took her to my shop than if I sent her in to her father, who was no friend of mine, and would scarce welcome me under his roof. So I lifted her, for the little scrap was as light as a kitten, and carried her down the street.

By now the whole crowd had perceived this new diversion, and the music had stopped. The neighbours, the musicians, Moll, the capering bear, and all, had abandoned their play and gathered round the fallen child. Despite my pleas to give her breathing space, they formed a close escort, murmuring sympathetic-ally as we passed along the street. I called to a neighbour child I knew to go summon the bonesetter who lived in the Strand, and she ran off with admirable speed, proud of her mission. But as I approached my door I heard behind me a mighty cry of "Stop! Give me my sinful child!" I turned to see Eliphalet, hastening out of his house, with a frown above his stark-white collar bands that would have curdled milk.

"I must tend to your child, sir," I called out, with all the courtesy I could muster, "for she is bleeding, and, I fear, broken."

"Do not take her through that door!" he commanded.

"Why then I must see to her out here in the street," I called back. I placed her on the table which in the weekdays served as my outdoor shop-board.

By this time Moll, the musicians, and the bear had pushed through the crowd for a closer look. Moll handed the beast's leading-strings to the young drummer, and came to my aid. I sent her to fetch certain necessaries from the shop. While she was about this business, the crowd parted again, this time to admit the child's father, with his other daughter close behind him. When the injured girl saw him she began to scream afresh, and I perceived that the presence of her devoted parent was no great comfort to her.

"Discipline!" he roared. "Discipline!" and I wondered what dire warning he imparted by this, until I remembered that Discipline was the poor babe's name.

"She fell out of your upper window," I said, "and I think her arm is broken, so I have summoned the bone-setter. In the meantime I will wash the dirt from her cuts, and feed her a cordial to dull the pain."

He thrust me aside, and set his furious face to hers. "Sinner!" he roared. "Sabbath breaker! What folly is this? What drew you away from the task I set you?"

"The bear's music, father," the child whispered.

"Music?" he scowled. "Pagan drums and cymbals? What needed you such trumpery trash when you had before you the true music of the Psalms?"

Moll emerged from the shop with a jug of water and a basin containing the things I'd asked for, then returned to her bear, who watched the proceedings as intently as the rest of the crowd.

As I washed the child's wounds and fed her spoonfuls of cordial, Eliphalet stood at her feet, scarce noticing my presence or the crowd's, so intent was he on berating her.

"You jezebel!" he screamed at the quivering infant, shaking his fist. "You wanton scarlet jade! Know ye the well-deserved punishments the Lord metes out to Sabbath breakers? Have I not recited to you the catalogue of such sinners and their fates? Know ye not of the vain housewife of Hogsden, who glanced wantonly in her looking-glass to admire herself on the

Lord's Day — and woke Monday morn to find her face eaten away in the night by a sudden leprosy? And what of the silly boy from Enfield, who perused a book of profane verse when he should have been reading his Bible, and found himself struck blind before the Sabbath was out? Have I not told you of the sea captain from Kent, who bethought to take advantage of a good wind and put to sea upon a sunny Sabbath morning — only to have a sudden storm come whistling up and break his ship all to pieces, with himself and all the poor sailors drowned in sight of land? And remember ye the little girl no older than you are, who dared to skip and caper upon the Lord's Day and danced all unseeing into the jaws of a hungry wolf? These are the well-deserved punishments awaiting sinners like yourself. Pray, my child, for forgiveness, and be thankful if no heavier torments fall upon you before the day is out!"

At this moment the bonesetter arrived. She was an old friend of mine (indeed, in earlier years, before Moll appeared, I'd wished her more than a friend, I do confess it), slim as a willow, but a good head taller than the ranting Eliphalet. She brushed him away like a troublesome gnat, and bent with me over the sobbing child. The father stood, scowling, then we heard him turn to the crowd and launch forth into an extempore sermon, which soon drove the onlookers back into their houses. Only Moll, her two musicians, and the dancing bear stood solemnly listening to his address, aside from the tear-stained twin sister, who still cowered at Eliphalet's heels, but seemed more interested in the bear's scratchings than in her father's wisdom.

The bonesetter finished her work, and bound up

young Discipline's arm in a clean cloth. Then she turned to address the glowering patriarch.

"Your daughter will need rest and quiet. Whatever she asks for to eat or drink, let her have, for the body knows its own needs in mending. Mistress Bridget will give you some syrups and potions, of which she must take a spoonful from each bottle every day, mingled up in a cup of blackcurrant cordial. I will come to her on Wednesday to see how her arm does. I will visit again, twice every week, and if all goes well, within two months her arm will be hale again. Young bones mend easily if care is taken with them."

"You presume too much, Mistress Bonesetter. How do you know that I will let you cross my threshold? I know little of your healing skill or of the apothecary's, but I know that the blessing of God is unlikely to fall upon the handiwork of wanton sinners and Sabbath-breakers, who ply their trades on the Lord's own day."

"Ply our trades?" I was incredulous. "Would you have your child lie broken and screaming until the morrow, when your pious scruples permit you to summon help?"

"If the child had not been so over full of wicked-ness and corruption she would have paid no heed to sounds of wanton mirth in a street of sinners, and would have bent her head over her assigned task. If the Lord saw fit to punish her by breaking her bones, then she must kiss the rod that smites her and bear her pains until the Lord sees fit to deliver her from it. Not only have you broken the Sabbath, but you have ministered to my child without my consent. As she is my charge and property, I'm sure any court would call it theft."

Moll, standing with her bear, grew incensed. "Theft? There's some would say the taking of babes from their mother is theft, Master Brown."

He sent her a black look. "I am their father," he replied coldly. "These children are rightfully mine."

Moll jeered, and held up her finger in the horned sign of the cuckold.

Eliphalet turned a shade of scarlet that was far too gaudy to be worn by sober Puritans.

"I care not whose child she is," said the bonesetter, losing patience. "But I demand the right to visit her and inspect the progress of her healing, lest the bone set crooked and she grow up a cripple."

"If that be the chastisement the Lord has assigned her," pronounced Eliphalet, "so be it. There is no call to interfere."

"Either you follow my directions for her care, and allow me access to your house," the bonesetter declared, "or I will keep the child myself until her arm has mended."

Brown pondered this. He clearly took little pleasure in the prospect of tending an invalid child, who would need more careful ministrations and more expensive feeding than was his custom to supply.

"If you take her," he warned, "I will pay not a groatsworth towards her keep."

"There will be no fees," replied the bonesetter. "I will happily provide her food and fire at my own expense, rather than entrust her to you. I would fear for her welfare at your hands."

"And should not I, her loving father, fear also for her welfare — to wit, the welfare of her soul? How do I know what moral infections may taint her in your sin-smirched household?"

"What calumny is this?" demanded the bonesetter, drawing herself up to her full height and glowering down at him. "I am as godly as you are, and if you doubt my spiritual worth, you have but to enquire of the vicar of St Bride's, who will satisfy you as to my piety."

"And who," thundered Eliphalet, "will satisfy me as to the piety of the vicar?" He launched forth into an attack on the corruption of the established church, which I cut short with a warning that the day was drawing in, and his wounded child might catch a dangerous chill.

"Take her!" he spat out. "And return her to me when her arm has fully mended, for she is of little use in my household in her present state. I will pray daily for her recovery, and that she be sent back to me uncorrupted."

I helped the bonesetter wrap little Discipline in a cloak, and she set off down the street, carrying the child, who had fallen asleep thanks to the soothing draught I'd given her.

Meanwhile her twin, Zeal-of-God, set up a terrible wail, as if she and not her sister were the injured one. It seemed she took no delight in the prospect of reigning as sole child in her father's house. He silenced her with a resounding slap, and led her away down the street.

But unbeknownst to Eliphalet, he had made a convert. The dancing bear, who had listened raptly to his sermonising, had apparently resolved to join his sect, for he broke free of Moll's grasp and ran after Eliphalet, who knew nothing of this until he felt a heavy paw on his backside. He turned to discover Ursinus at his heels. The bear, overjoyed at such proximity to his new found prophet, embraced Eliphalet with an effectionate hug, at which display of loyalty the Puritan began to howl for succour. But the bear, undeterred, spun his favourite round in a merry dance much to the delight of those folk who still lingered in their doorways.

"For shame!" bellowed one old woman. "Dancing on the Sabbath, Eliphalet?"

Moll and her minions ambled down the street in leisurely pursuit. The bear, as Moll shouted to Eliphalet, was only trying to be friends. Still, she signalled to the two musicians, who struck up a tune that the bear recognised as his customary call to home and supper. He basely deserted his Puritan friend, and stopped in his tracks, contemplating a return to his guardians, and presumably also to the Established Church.

"Fear him not!" Moll called to Eliphalet, who was dragging his daugher angrily across the threshold, "for he's only a kind of cousin to your children, bringing greetings from his stepmother, your departed wife, who dwells at the Bear Garden." And once more she made the sign of the cuckold as the furious Eliphalet banged shut the door behind him.

"I don't think he loves us too well," Moll observed, after she succeeded in consoling the snuffling bear, who still sent longing looks towards Eliphalet's door. "But then it hardly seems he loves his children either, so unmoved is he by his daughter's injury."

"I'm sure he loves them, after his own fashion," I said. "But he reminds me of those travellers' tales I've heard, about a foreign Switzer city where these Puritans hold sway. There the citizens punish disobedient children by hanging, with the full consent of their loving parents, who believe such earthly penalties are for the betterment of their babes' immortal souls."

"Well then, let Bleak-face Brown go bide in Switzerland," said Moll. "But for my part I'll stop here. Our English hangings are good enough for me."

"No doubt our neighbour Brown thinks you good enough for English hanging. But tell me, how did you come by the dancing bear? I hope you don't plan to keep it. If so, you may choose between its company tonight and mine."

"Borrowed for a wager," said Moll, "and expected back at the Bear Garden within the hour."

YOUNG Discipline's arm soon mended, and she was to be seen once again with her sister, trailing meekly at her father's heels. But where once she would have stared at me in terror, and averted her eyes, now (if her father's back was turned) she smiled and winked in a most irreverent fashion. Once, in secret, she tiptoed into the shop and handed me a sticky fistful of sweetmeats. But her father, whenever he deigned to look my way, only glared and scowled. I feared he was studying some way to do me harm.

But all such concerns were cast aside the night Moll rushed in from the tavern all agog, with Baby sending forth her piercing wolf-howls of delight.

"I have news," Moll announced, "from the tavern."

"News?" I asked. "What news? That beer is made from hops? That drunkards have red noses? That Mother Bunch waters her ale — save the special barrel she keeps for friends in her back parlour?"

"I bring news," she declared, "of a play."

"I wish instead you'd brought news of a beefsteak pie. For it's your turn to bring home the supper, and I'm fair dying of hunger."

"If you can stave off your pangs and hear me out, I'll

bring you home a fine roast capon in celebration."

"Celebration of what?"

"Celebration of the comedy that my good friends and boozing companions Middleton and old Tom Dekker are making ready."

"What cause is that for celebration? A new comedy pours out of their pens every month."

"But this comedy is different," she said smugly. "This one is titled *The Roaring Girl*, and I, your very own Moll, am the hero of the piece."

I was, for once, stunned speechless.

"The bravest player in the company is to speak my part — and I am to sit in a place of honour on the night of its first enactment at the Fortune."

"What wild fancies will they tell of you?"

"None so wild as the truth, Mistress Bridget," she replied, clipping me in a rib-cracking embrace. "But who cares for such minor matters as the truth? My lifelong dream has, by roundabout means, come true — and Mad Moll walks upon the stage at last!"

In the days that followed, before the new comedy was mounted, Moll was closemouthed about her conversations with the playwrights, and scarce dropped a hint of the story to be told. I realised this was because she knew little of it. Her friend Middleton was wise enough to tell her nothing, fearing she might take unexpected offence, and break his pate with her staff.

Although some of Moll's player-friends knew of our friendship, as did our nearest neighbours, the world at large, though well-versed in Moll's exploits, knew nothing of my connections with her — and we preferred to keep it so. For this reason I thought it best that she sit alone with the playwrights in her place of honour. I would mingle obscurely with the crowd, having Mother Bunch and old Mavis to bear me company.

But when the night of the comedy arrived, I was called to assist the midwife at a neighbour's lying-in, and the girl's pains came on sooner than expected. So Mavis and I passed the night helping the midwife. The girl was scarce fourteen, and so small and ill-nourished that the midwife said it was a mercy that the babe came early and undersized. Withal it was a tiring travail, and I was home just before sunrise, to find our bed empty and no sign of Moll.

I was not perturbed. The play, I knew, would be only the first act in a long night's revelry, which was likely to be in full fling even now at Mother Bunch's. But I was tired, and felt no urge to rush through the dark streets to join in at the rump end of Moll's festivities. So I lay down for a few hours' sleep, and then went off to Chick Lane in search of Moll.

I found Mother Bunch cheerfully clearing the debris of the long night's hard drinking, which she, it seemed, had presided over all unscathed. Moll lay in a crumpled heap on a bench in the corner, fast asleep.

"I'll rouse her for you," offered Mother Bunch, whistling merrily as she flung the slops from her scrubbing-bucket over my snoring love. But Moll only moaned, and rolled away from the shower, landing with a thump on the floor. Baby lay exhausted underneath the bench, and so bleary were the eyes she raised at the disturbance that I defy anyone to tell me that mastiffs don't get drunk.

"My mid-day customers will soon be upon us," said Mother Bunch. "You'd better move her. Upstairs to her old chamber, I think. You'll never get her home, the state she's in."

Knowing Moll would never make it out the door, where the sunshine would torment her scarlet eyes and the birdsong fall like hammer-blows upon her head, I coaxed Moll to her feet and up the stairs.

I dropped her down upon her old pallet, and she pulled me down beside her in a spirituous embrace.

"I thought you said your head and belly were cast-iron proof against drunkenness," I chided her. "You always vow you can drink all comers under the table."

"Well I can and I did," she retorted, "save good Mother Bunch who is as well-pickled as an old beer barrel and scarce notices whether she's drunk or not."

"I'm hungry to hear how it went at the playhouse."

"Hungry!" she moaned. "Alas, I shall never be hungry again. Oh, my belly. Oh, my head!"

But Mother Bunch came in with a steaming jug of the foul-smelling brew she called Morning's Repentance, whose ingredients she would never reveal to me, save that it contained a copious quantity of mustard. She stood over Moll, ignoring her protests, and forced her to drain every drop, punctuated though they were by Moll's cries of pain.

By the time Mother Bunch went away with the jug, and returned bearing a tray of bread, cheese and ale, Moll had been magnificently sick and was nearly herself again, a traveller returned from Sot's Purgatory. She thought she could manage a healing tobacco-pipe, and said she'd try a morsel of bread and cheese. When she had wolfed down three-quarters of the loaf and most of the cheese, she felt herself sufficiently hale to recount for me the events at the playhouse.

IT'S passing strange to see a shadow of yourself, or what others deem the likeness of yourself, walk before you on the stage — doing deeds you never did and saying words that, for the most part, are a poet's words and not your own. I confess I was somewhat fearful at the prospect, most unlike myself, when I met Middleton and Tom Dekker in the tavern in Whitecross Street, hard by the Fortune. They plied me with drink. I suspected they were trying to make me drunk, so I might cheerfully accept whatever calumnies I saw enacted upon the stage. I perceived in them a kind of skittishness, which fuelled my suspicions further. So, when a few more cups of good canary had given me a false Dutchman's courage, I charged them with my doubts. I said there must be something they feared would anger me, or they would not chew so vigorously upon the points of their collars and upon their fingertips.

They confessed they dreaded my misliking the play, and said they had sought to shape a comedy that would please the crowds without displeasing me. They explained their unease as a common disease of playmakers, when they see their cherished infant exposed to the mercies of the actors and the crowd.

So I promised I'd take their picture of me in good

part, as long as there was no slander in it, and they said that — if anything — they feared I might protest at being painted too virtuous and saintly.

I replied this promised to be a fantastical play indeed, that would show roaring Moll on the side of the angels. How would I know her when she came upon the stage?

They said I would know her by her dress, her bravery, and even some of her words, and with this reassurance they led me into the playhouse.

They carried me to a seat at the very side of the stage. I felt as if they were leading me to the block to be dismembered and strung up for a traitor. But I heard the roars and cheers from many hundreds of throats, and looked out to see the crowd hallooing at me as I came up. The blood rose in me, and my sanguine humour was restored; I took off my hat and waved it to them, and for the joy of it I cut a caper and turned a somerset as was my ancient custom. Then Middleton and Dekker, my jailers still, saw fit to restrain me and lead me to my seat, to let the comedy begin.

I will not unfold the tale to you in its entirety, lest you be wearied of it before you have seen it for yourself — but I promise you it is the strangest mixture of the Moll you know and a Moll that never was nor could be.

Alas, I am not the whole of the comedy, for Dekker tells me there must needs be a plot to carry both players and spectators along. Even the sight of a figure as remarkable as Moll will not suffice to satisfy an audience that has paid for three hours of diversion.

I was sore impatient to see myself, for there were lengthy matters of cruel fathers, betrothals, disguises and deceptions in the first act, before I at last saw that creature I must perforce call myself. I laughed and howled and fell upon the ground in merriment, as did the whole of the audience. For instead of having one of the piping-voiced boy players, who commonly take the women's parts, to personate me, I had for my actor the biggest, beefiest player in the company, with a bellowing loud voice and hands like huge York hams and a manner like a snorting stag — he commonly acts the parts of kings and murderers.

It was full five minutes before the crowd quietened down to let him speak. Tom Dekker looked at me sidelong, fearful that I might take offence at this conceit. But I liked it well, and told him I would have been sore affronted if they had chosen instead some silly squeaking-voiced youth who commonly figures forth women sillier and stupider than any woman ever was in life.

And this he or she, or was it I, was a brave one indeed, and fought duels, saved debtors from the sergeants, outwitted cheaters, turning thieves nips away from my friends' purses, and even singing a song in the thieves' Latin. But most important, I rescue youths from the folly and tyranny of their parents, and work a most ingenious ploy with a young man seeking to frighten his father, by announcing that he wishes to take the Roaring Girl to wife. But this is all feigned to help to poor swain to marry another lady, which match his greedy father forbids because her family's fortune isn't large enough.

When I saw that this was the turn the plot was taking, I shouted out that I would help no woman put her neck on the nuptial chopping block, no matter how fair her suitor. But Middleton clapped his hand over my mouth and bid me hush and said I would have my say on this very subject later on. And indeed she did pronounce upon the way men treat women, and how I viewed marriages and why she never would marry — and it struck me suddenly that her words, though poetically turned and twisted, were like those I spoke to Sly and Middleton the night I turned up the high German by the heels. And, oh, indeed, that was in the play too, for she says, "Yes, I have turned up those of the high German's size by the heels before now," and all the crowd cheered and shouted. I stood up and took a bow, for that deed of mine is still a famous tale in London. But Dekker, fearing I might delay the action further, tugged my jerkin so hard I nearly tumbled down. I would have called him out for it, disturbing me in my moment of glory — but I was eager to see if certain plots hatched against me would come to anything, or if I was to be hanged or murdered. So I let it pass.

And, in truth, the comedy ended with the good rewarded, the greedy punished, and Moll triumphant. She said she'd vow to marry on the day when Honesty and Truth's unslandered, and Woman manned but never pandered. Which as everyone understands, means Never. Which may not be to the letter what I said in that long-ago alehouse quarrel, but it is near enough to the spirit of the thing, and I am content.

Then it was ended and everyone cheered, and the players made me rise and take a bow with them, and everyone roared for Roaring Moll. And I was carried back into the tiring-house, which smelled of sweat and face-paint. All the actors jostled together, stripping themselves of their stage clothes and vying with each other to be first to reach their favourite tavern. And I was carried off from the playhouse on the actors' shoulders, and we all visited a large number of boozing kens, more than I can recall, finishing off at Mother Bunch's. And it was a glorious night, although I had to chide Middleton and Dekker both for certain points in their text I chose to quarrel with. But by the end of the night we were friends again, and I doubt they'll remember where their black eyes came from anyway.

So in short it was a wondrous time, and I'm sorry you weren't there to share it with me. Yet Fame has her price as well as her pleasures, for though I am well-known abroad, there are certain enterprises of mine which thrive best on discretion and obscurity. So I fear I must now for a time put aside some of my accustomed trades, and take up some other occupation until the fickle public finds itself another idol. Some new talking brazen head will be found, or a mermaid come over from the Virginias, or some other nine days' wonder will supplant me as the apple of the common eye.

*Moll Cutpurse*     "GIVE up your trade!" I said, amazed and delighted. For I often feared Moll would end up on a rope before I was ready to relinquish her.

"Not forever, mind, not forever. But there is one

new enterprise, less risky than my usual work, that I think may please and profit me for a time."

"What enterprise is this?" I asked.

"Let me speak of it later, for I am much recovered from this morning's malady, and I feel a mighty hunger come upon me. So let us go forth and find ourselves a few jugged hares, or the side of an ox well-roasted, and I shall tell you of my prospects over nuncheons."

SITTING among the bones of our feast in the Saracen's Head, I pressed Moll to tell me of her projected undertaking.

"Fortunetelling," she replied.

"Fortunetelling? You?" I laughed. "Where does this curious notion spring from?"

"What's so curious about it? Do you doubt my competence?"

"Sweetest Moll, I wouldn't doubt your competence for any task on earth, but I fear you are hardly equipped to go future-hunting among the stars. You have but a layman's simple knowledge of the Zodiac, you lack the Latin needed to consult the ancient books, and though many coins, both real and counterfeit, pass through your hands, you are all at sea among the higher mysteries of numbers — without which no proper prognostication can be made. So, failing all these skills, how can you hope for customers?"

"In fortunetelling, as with your own arts, Bridget, results are everything. If I can help but one merchant to a successful venture, or reveal to one lady the whereabouts of her missing glove, word of my success will spread. All the curious citizens of London will flock to my door. I have no ambition to be a figure

185

flinger: I shall leave the scanning of birth-charts to mathematical wizards. There may be those among the public who do indeed prefer their mysteries made more mysterious by the admixture of a little scholarly hokery-pokery — dusty tomes from the past that hold the secrets of the future in their mouldering pages, but all in Greek, alas, all in Greek. These aficionados are not the clients I expect; my custom will be among those ordinary folk who ask ordinary questions."

"And how can you hope to answer even ordinary questions?"

"I'm not totally unschooled in these murky arts. Remember, I once sat at the feet of the Gypsy Queen. And though my sojourn with her was brief, I learned many things, that have remained locked up these many years in a back-parlour of my memory-house. My knowledge may have gathered dust, but it's still of perfect soundness."

In my heart of hearts I remained an unbeliever. But not for the world would I dissuade Moll from any occupation that would distance her from the smoke of the branding-iron or the shadow of the gallows.

"But where will you do your scrying? Will you carry a gazing-crystal from fair to fair?"

"Indeed not. I shall have a proper shop. Do you know Mother Broughton, who reads fortunes in Chick Lane, hard by Mother Bunch's? She is going away into the country to visit her brother, and wants someone to keep her trade and her premises warm. So Mother Bunch put my name to her as a likely prospect. She laughed at first, but goody Bunch persuaded her I had great untapped gifts and knew all the secrets of the Egyptians. So she is content with our arrangement, for if all else fails I'll keep her shop well-aired and fired in her absence. And if I prove a poor prophet, her clients will be all the happier when she returns."

"Will you wear a turban and a wizard's robes all sewn with stars and symbols?"

"Mother Bunch said I should bedeck myself as a foreign Egyptian and none would know it was me. But Middleton says he thinks I'll fare best as plain Moll, in my customary hose and doublet. He says that he'll call anyone a fool who sneers at my fortunetellings. He told me that the cleverest seer as ever lived was thought by some to be half-man, half-woman, for he passed part of his life as one sex and part as the other."

"Tiresias?"

"Yes, that was it. Some dead foreigner. Middleton thinks perhaps I will be another such as him, with a gift for prophecy; because of what he deems my admixture of male and female."

"And what said you to that?"

"I smote him for it. I said there was nothing male in me, for I set my sights higher, and could better any man at his own game."

"What said he to that?"

"When he picked himself up out of the dirt he begged my pardon, and said he referred but to my admixture of feminine sex and masculine attire. So he bought me the next round of drinks in recompense, and we were at peace."

MOLL embarked on her new enterprise a few days later, when Mistress Broughton went away into the country. But by then I too was out of London, for I'd promised my Aunt Mary a long visit down in Kent. I had to wait until my return, some four weeks later, for news of Moll's venture. Aunt Mary laughed long and loud to think of Moll as a shopkeeper, sitting behind her board awaiting customers. But much as I delighted in my old aunt's company, and enjoyed the sweet peace of the country, I was impatient to return to Moll, for we had never spent so many nights apart since my long-ago sojourn in my aunt's old cottage, when I never knew if I would see my roaring love again.

Although I expected to find a locked shop and a cold, empty house on my return, with Moll busy at Chick Lane, I came home to discover a welcoming fire, a laden table, and Moll crouched by the hearth, heating a warming-pan to take the chill off our bed.

"I thought you'd be at Chick Lane," I said between kisses, "for I never told you when to expect me."

"You can have no secrets from a seer," she replied mysteriously.

"How goes your fortunetelling?"

"Sit down to your supper and I'll tell you all about it. There's a pie from Pie Corner and kickshaws from the pastry-cook."

"And while I'm eating that, you can taste Aunt Mary's honey, which she sends you with much love. Also, there's a ham and some cherry preserves from Mother Bunch's sister, and a crock of goose fat we're to rub on our chests in the winter, and some beeswax candles and a good stock of roots and powders for my medicine chest (with more coming up next week by the carrier). Also, a pair of woollen hose Aunt Mary knitted for you, and gloves for us both. Oh yes, and a fine plum-cake the pair of them baked together, quarrelling all the while about the quantity of fruit, the choice of spices, the time of baking and several bottles of elderberry wine."

"So the two old Joans still get on well together?"

"Busier than the bees they tend so lovingly, quarrelling happily about the proper way to distill and pickle the brew. Both of them send you love and wish you well, and beg I send them word by the carrier about your new enterprise."

"Well, let us unpack these country delights, and I will tell you of my venture in the arts of prophecy."

I THOUGHT, when first I came into Mistress Broughton's shop, I'd have to sit solitary, muttering into her crystal to conjure up customers. But, thanks to Mother Bunch's good services as a vendor of news, word of my new occupation sped quickly through the city. So I opened my door at the first knock, and found a great crowd of petitioners awaiting me. I'd thought that fortunetelling would be, in comparison to my usual business, a quiet life, making these few weeks a half-holiday. But it seemed that most of the young bravos of the city, and even more of the maidens, not to mention the merchants, the housewives, and a dozen members of the thieves' fraternity, were all impatient to have their fortunes told and their dreams interpreted, and would consult no other seer but the

*Moll's Tale*

189

new one in Chick Lane. Upon closer scrutiny I discovered that it was less a wish to know their fortunes than a wish to have a close look at Roaring Moll that brought them forward. But I bethought myself that if they were willing to part with their money for such a purpose, then it mattered not if I was a good prophet or not, for until the novelty wore off I was assured of a healthy income.

By the end of the first week this crowd of curiosity-seekers diminished, and people who genuinely sought my help came forward in greater numbers. This pleased me well, for I was eager to cut my teeth in the trade, and to see if the old gypsy's skills were of any use.

I dispensed with Mother Broughton's crystal and her star charts, the first because I deemed it jiggery-pokery, the second because I knew not how to read them. Instead I used a pack of ancient greasy cards, whose secrets were first taught to me by my gypsy queen, and certain other arts of which I'll speak more anon. I feared at first that some would try me with trick questions — "What will the weather be on Wednesday next?" — and others that would trip me up in short order. But I found no such traps laid for me. My petitioners, in the main, fell into four common kinds. First, those who came to me on matters of love and lust — youths and maidens, old as well as young, eager innocents wanting to know who they would marry. Also, their adulterous elders, bent on games of cuckoldry in the suburbs. For the young ones, I studied the lines of their palms, told them to heed their own hopes and likings, warning them to be on their guard, think twice, and beware of churches. For the others, I know not what they hoped from me, but I sent many an old lecher away with a flea in his ear.

The second sort of questioner sought to discover the success of some large enterprise: "Should I set out for the Virginia colonies?" "Should I purchase land in Suffolk?" "Should I trust my wife's brother with my money?" For such enquiries as these, I carefully perused my magic cards, and delivered such cryptic messages as they provided me, well-wrapped in riddles that could equally well mean yea or nay to any question. Thus no one could tax me with deceiving them.

The third part of my customers were those who came to have dreams explained, a task which pleases me greatly. For I am of a questioning humour, and would as soon peep into my neighbour's inmost thoughts as under her skirts to know what mysteries do lie there. Some say our dreams are pictures of the future; others perceive them to be windows into our hearts. But in either case, it would surprise you to know the curious comedies that are played upon the pillows of our citizens: an old woman dreams of her dead children, carrying the moon in a basket; a pregnant wife dreams she gives birth to a two-headed dog; a kitchen-maid dreams, night after night, that she is lost in a glorious rose-garden. She asks no interpretation of her dreams, but only begs to know some trick that will keep her there, and stave off the morning with its greasy pots and trenchers. Alas, I couldn't help her, and told her only that I hoped she might find some way out of her servitude. She said she saw no escape, save marriage, which would only send her to a meaner kitchen. I told her of my own flight from the same labours, but she said ruefully that such daring ploys were not for her. So I wished her well and gave her back her penny . . .

Hard on her heels there came a sailor's wife, much troubled. She told me her husband passed two and three years at a time away at sea. I advised her that she must not be frightened by dreams of storm and shipwreck, for dreams, as mirrors of life, do often show things back to front. If they pictured danger at sea they might indeed signify the opposite, telling her that the voyage prospered and her husband's ship was safe.

"I never dream of dangers at sea," she replied, "for, in truth, when he's away I scarcely think of him. I like my solitude, and my cat for my closest companion, and if it had been otherwise I would never have married a sailor. When he comes home we get on well enough, and I love to hear his tales of strange lands and barbarous places, but within a few weeks the pair of us grow restless, and are both well-pleased when he finds another ship.

"This last time he came back with a tale that struck me strangely. He'd been on a voyage to Constantinople for carpets and spices. He told me that on a great height above the harbour there he spied a most wonderful palace. He discovered that this was the place where the Soldan, king over all the terrible Turks, keeps his wives. There are many hundreds of them dwelling there, all dressed in rich silks and bathed in rare perfumes. They live all crowded together in a paradise of gardens and fountains that no man save the Soldan is allowed to see. Even the slaves who guard the place have been unmanned by gelding, lest they interfere with his women. Some of the ladies are his honest wives, lawfully wed according to their pagan custom, others are the spoils of war, or gifts from other princes who seek his favour. He has so many women that he is hard pressed to remember them, and it is said that among them all he calls only a few favourites to his bed, leaving the rest to languish. Yet he is a miser with these treasures, and will part with none of them, which enforces upon these neglected ladies a perpetual chastity. But it is whispered abroad that these women do embroil themselves in intrigues and amorous passions, and do practise secret arts by which they pleasure each other as thoroughly as any man could hope to.

"Now this was only one of many stories that my husband told me after his last voyage, for it was a journey crammed with incident, and he passed quickly to other matters — an escape from pirates, a giant dolphin, a near-shipwreck in the Bay of Biscay. But the thought of those women in the Turk's palace began to haunt me.

"My husband found another ship, bound for the Virginias for tobacco, and in the days before he sailed I was far too busy making and mending, packing and provisioning, to think of anything save the necessary contents of his sea-chest. On the night of his leave-taking when, as was his custom, he rogered me, I found myself thinking all the while of these Turkish ladies. And for the whole of this month I have suffered strange dreams. I dreamed I stood in St Paul's, where a woman, veiled and hooded, beckoned to me from behind a pillar. I dreamed I walked naked through an orchard whose trees were heavy with blossom, and butterflies with women's faces fluttered round my breasts. Then I dreamed I lay in the centre of a great fountain, and the water leapt up in a high arc out of my womb, and two Turkish ladies came to the fountain and stripped off their silken robes and danced in my waters.

"I rise up, aching with longing, unsure whether to shun sleep or welcome it, that such tantalizing visions loom up and fret me. I know not what such dreams foretell, nor how I should cure myself of them, or if I should want to. I have heard that you are wise in such matters, and I shall be forever in your debt if you can enlighten me."

I knew not if she meant that I was wise in the matter of reading dreams, or wise in the matter of lusting after women, but I saw she was sore vexed and I strove to speak carefully. I wished you had been there to help me. I asked her if she had never heard before of such things happening, for women making love together was not simply some foreign barbarity, but did occur everywhere, even here in London. She was much amazed by this, but I said such love of like to like must be as old as the world. She asked why then it was so little known, and I told her this was like as not by design of men, who being jealous that a woman might get her pleasure without submitting to them, would strive to keep the very notion of such things from infecting the ears of their wives and daughters.

"But what," she asked, "do women do together?"

And she cast me such a meaning-laden look that I knew she wanted me to teach her there and then. She was a lovely creature indeed, but not to my taste, even were I one for straying. Nor was I prepared to abuse my client's trust. There are plenty of prophets who would — like the goatish Doctor Foreman, who holds a woman's hand on pretext of reading her palm-lines, gazes deep into her eyes, saying that the stars therein yield up more meaning than the stars of her birth-chart, and otherwise tickles her longings until he has tumbled her.

So I merely told her that in time she would likely meet a woman or women she wished to lie with, and would discover the other to be in agreement, and her body's own desires would then be her guide. She asked what if she never found one, and I promised her that now she knew what she sought she was bound to discover others like-minded.

"And if not," I said, "you have your cherished solitude, and your dreams of Turkish ladies, who can be bidden to visit you through your mind's eye and your own cunning fingers. Don't disparage such ghostly visitations, for there are times in life that we have nothing else to live on."

She seemed much cheered by this, so I kissed her on the lips — chastely, my jealous darling, chastely — wished her well, and let her go.

But of all my custom, the fourth and most profitable part comes from those seeking news of lost and stolen goods. For these commissions I need no tools of wizardry, but only the help of loyal disciples, who bring me intelligence of every theft in London, and news of which receivers are holding the missing goods. So when some wealthy citizen comes to me in search of his watch or his jewel-case I am able to help him to a swift reunion with his stolen treasures, in recompense for a generous fee. Which I then divide between myself and the receiver, not forgetting a coin for my young officers besides. Although it's but three weeks since my first such miraculous recovery (a pair of silver candlesticks (filched from an open window in Holborn), I have already built up a thriving trade. The prosperous victims of these disappearances are no fools, and know that I am likely to render a fast return for the money they pay me.

But such enterprises need care to run smoothly. The return of stolen items is a delicate business. As a soothsayer I may discover where missing property lies, but I must not myself receive it, and those shadowy brokers who hold the goods must not be named lest they be implicated in the theft. So I've deemed it convenient to nominate some secret place, such as the hollow of an old tree in Finsbury Field, or under the hearth-bricks of a derelict house, where my clients may be sent to find their missing property. One of my young officers secretly precedes them there, slips the goods into the hiding hole, and hides nearby to watch over the treasure.

I'm well satisfied with these arrangements now, but in the first days there were some slips and one true disaster. A foolish youth, one of my more backward pupils, stole a watch. Instead of carrying it to the receiver, he delivered it straight to me, not understanding my part in the business. I berated him, and directed him towards the broker by means of a boot up his backside. But alas some busybody constable had pursued him from the place whence the watch was taken, and saw him through my window, placing the blasted object on my shop-board. So he whistled up his fellows and within an instant apprehended myself and the stupid youth, naming him a thief and me a receiver. They carried us off to the Counter in a cart, and my oafish companion was hauled away, kicking and screaming, and I never saw more of him. I hope they flogged him till his bones showed.

I was led up to a table, in a great draughty hall,

where some greasy clerk wrote my name in a book, and asked me how much I could afford to fee the gaoler. For the Counter is a holding place for all manner and means of prisoners. Ragged nips awaiting their noses slit or their foreheads branded lie starving in stinking dungeons. Nearby, rich debtors lodge in well-furnished chambers, nibbling upon the delicates their friends send in to them; they pay the gaolers a fat fee for such comforts. I knew that if I wished to eat while I awaited the attentions of the magistrates, then I had to fee my keepers. But so swiftly had I been hauled away by the constables that I had no coin about me.

The swinish clerk advised me, with an oily leer, that it was possible for penniless prisoners to barter the clothes upon their backs as payment. I would have broken his head had his lackeys not restrained me. But I stood my ground and said I would pay nothing, as my friends would soon succour me. For I knew that Mother Bunch would by now have news of my captivity, and I prayed she would think to send in food and money. The foul clerk seemed sore put out by this, and said he wished he was the Bridewell beadle, for I was one whore he'd like to have the whipping of.

Before I could leap to tear out his throat with my bare hands, which I could have done as easily as dispatching a chicken, I saw the constable who had arrested me rush in, distressed and red-faced. He whispered to a gaoler who whispered to his fellow who whispered to the clerk, who shrugged and spat.

"Alas, Mistress Frith," he said, "it seems we are not to have the pleasure of entertaining you. Get out."

I wasted no time in foolish questions, but hastily departed, following one of the gaolers, who — like the prince in the old story — led me out of this Hell. When

I was safely on the street again, and he lingered on the terrible threshold, I made bold to ask him what caused this sudden change in my fortunes. He replied that the constable had discovered, to his shame, that the evidence was missing. It seems the wallet wherein he'd placed the stolen watch was nipped from his belt by the hand of a pickpocket. So I knew my friends had come to my aid after all.

*Moll Cutpurse*   MOLL did most of her roaring and raving in streets far from the one we lived in. She brawled in Gray's Inn Fields, caroused in the suburbs, passed her false coin in Southwark or Cheapside, told her fortunes and trained up her young pupils in Chick Lane, and received her secret intelligences in taverns and ordinaries throughout the city. We lived peacefully among our neighbours, save for Eliphalet Brown. We had our occasional skirmishes with him, for his expropriation of my father's shop-goods and my insistence on treating his injured child were but the opening salvoes in a long struggle. In time our dealings with him blossomed into a citizen's War of the Roses, dividing all who dwelt nearby into two separate camps.

In the early days, when Brown was an interloper,

coming down like a carrion-crow over the plague-pits, the neighbourhood viewed him with suspicion and contempt. But over the years he succeeded in buying the leaseholds to most of the houses in the quarter, and hounded their inhabitants with demands for ever-rising rents. Because I had inherited the freehold of my own shop from my father, Brown could neither squeeze money out of us nor drive us from the neighbourhood, so instead he thought to drown me in a sea of litigation. He brought writs against me for Sabbath-breaking, for creating noisome odours by distilling drugs in my back-shop, and similar complaints. But these attacks were no more than flea-bites, and usually came to nothing, with Eliphalet laughed out of court. Moll was all for rounding up a crowd of her unsavoury comrades to chase him out of the neighbourhood once and for all. But I reminded her that most of the houses in our street were now occupied by the pious sectaries he'd planted there. If we valued our peace and my prosperity, we'd best be circumspect. However, we were forever on our guard for opportunities whereby we might safely plague him.

One night, when Moll had been a zealous scholar in a drinking-academy at the Devil's Tavern, she came stumbling through the door, whistling and singing, bearing a large, mysterious bundle wrapped up in her cloak. When I held out a candle to light her up the stairs and into bed, I saw that the bundle squirmed and struggled in her arms, and discovered that the noise I heard was not Moll breaking wind, but strange sounds of protest from underneath her cloak.

"Not a word," she warned, and carried her burden up to our chamber. She deposited it on a heap of old

199

rags and straw in the corner, where her mastiff slept at night. She unwrapped the heaving parcel to reveal a great swollen-bellied pregnant sow.

"You naughty thief!" I cried. "That's Eliphalet's pig!"

"Alas," she said, "coming home through the lane from my merry-making, I stumbled over this lady in the darkness. She squealed and told me she was sore affronted. I thought that I should make amends to her for the insult, so I carried her here, to enjoy our hospitality during her lying-in, which I think is imminent."

And, to be sure, with a great heave and a mighty groan, the sow began to deliver forth her litter. In a little while she lay content among a family of fine piglets.

"We can hardly keep her," I said to Moll.

"I wouldn't think on it," she replied, "for that would be thievery. Tomorrow, when she has had time to rest, I'll let the lady out by the garden gate, which returns her to her customary stamping ground. But, as for her progeny, they were born under our roof and in our care, so I see no reason why old Brown should think himself their grandsire."

The next day, when Eliphalet set out in search of the pregnant sow he'd last seen rootling in his neighbour's carrot patch (which depredations never troubled him unduly, as long as the garden was not his own), he found instead a much thinner creature. But however much he pressed her, she kept mum as to where she'd dropped the cargo he'd hoped to profit by. He scrutinised the houses round about, closely sniffing the smoke from our chimney to see if there issued forth a smell of roast suckling pig. But Moll kept her adopted infants snug by the fire, spoon-feeding them on warm milk. In a few days she carried them forth to Smithfield (discreetly, in a covered basket), where she sold them for a good price.

Although he had no evidence against us, Eliphalet believed that any bad luck he encountered was likely to be the result of our efforts. He bided his time for revenge, and soon found an opportunity.

Moll, as always, came and went as she pleased, and I was happy to spend any solitary evenings mixing simples for my shop or studying alchemical texts. But one night I became worried at Moll's long absence. Promptitude was never her greatest virtue, but on this night she had promised to be home at sunset with the makings of our supper, and when the bells struck ten she had still not appeared. I went across to enquire after her at the Globe, and they said they'd seen nothing of her since noontime, when she and some scribbler friend of hers had disturbed the peace of the house with their drunken debates. The quarrel, it seemed, was over the sect called the Family of Love, and whether these, and other strange cults, could ever be countenanced. Such amiable, if noisy, quarrels were nothing unusual in the course of Moll's day, and I went back home with no further clue to her disappearance. I ate a meagre, lonely supper of stale bread and dried-out cheese, for I was at this time too preoccupied with my alchemical experiments to bother with ordinary cook-pots. I went to bed in a foul temper, certain that Moll had been carried off to some playhouse or pleasure-garden, forgetful of her promise to honour my birthday with a fine roast capon.

Some time later I was shaken from sleep by a banging and rattling at the wooden shutters in the back-shop. I seized a heavy candlestick, for there had been reports of robbers in the neighbourhood. Moll's aged mastiff, who was asleep at the foot of our bed, never stirred. I fear she was more bred to abetting crimes than preventing them. I crept down the dark stairs to the room behind my shop, whose windows overlooked an alleyway inhabited by a vast tribe of cats. As usual, I'd barred the shutters before going to bed, but the thief was pushing hard at them, and he must have been a strong brute for they strained and looked as if they'd soon be in splinters. Summoning up my courage I called out to the intruder in the boldest voice I could muster: "Come no further, you rogue, for I have a flask of acid that I will fling in your face, that will burn your eyes and nose away. And further-more, this is Moll Cutpurse's own house, and if you disturb it there will be no haven for you until she comes with her minions and tears your arms from their sockets."

The pounding stopped, and I began to warm to my task, listing all the punishments that any thief who violated her house was like to suffer at Moll's hands. Then there was silence, and I prayed that the intruder had given up and gone, though I would not be so rash as to unbar the shutters and find out. Then I heard through the wooden panels the sound of choked and muffled laughter, and Moll's voice boomed out, "What I will do to that thief is but a mere shadow of what I will do to thee, my lady, if you don't unbar this window and let me in."

Throwing open the shutters, I stood back while she clambered over the sill.

"What's wrong with the door?" I asked in a frost-bitten voice.

"Light the lamp and see."

When I did so I saw Moll in a most bedraggled state, with her best velvet cloak all torn and muddied, her breeches in rags, her feather hat missing, and the broadsword gone from her scabbard. Her face was a parti-coloured tapestry of cuts and bruises. Seeing her thus, I forgot all my anger at her broken promise, and quickly brought ointments and water to cleanse her wounds. As she stripped off her sadly-ruined finery, she told me what had befallen her.

I WAS on my way to the Leadenhall to buy you a fine, fresh capon. My journey took me past St Antling's churchyard, which seemed, at first glance, to be all aswarm with huge black beetles. But as I came up to it, I saw it was but a meeting of Puritan sectaries, gathered together to listen to some windy sermoniser. Now earlier today I was entered into a dispute with someone who claimed these sectaries are not all such hypocrites as old Eliphalet. He said there may be grains of truth in what they preach, and that some of the ideals they aspire to might better the lot of poor men here on earth as well as in heaven. So I thought, when I encountered a nest of them, that I should hear for myself what they preached, for let it never be said that I am narrow-minded.

So I went into the back of the church, in time to hear the lecturer announce his theme: he would preach upon the Judgment Day soon to come upon us, and would enlighten the congregation as to the joys that await those the Lord has chosen. Not least among these joys is watching sinners and scoffers dragged screaming down to the flames of Hell. He spoke in long words, and rambled greatly in his discourse, and I soon found that I had lost the thread of his argument.

I diverted myself by looking at the people around me: fat merchants and their wives, whose clothes were dark and sober, but made of the costliest cloth. They were all so well-fed that scarce four of them could crowd upon a bench that would easily seat half-a-dozen poorer folk. I saw tradesmen with mouths like tightly-drawn purses, among them that infamous baker who was lately drawn through the town at the cart's tail for selling underweight loaves. I saw sober-sided greybeards leering goatishly at maidens young enough to be their grand-daughters, even shifting secretly in their seats for a better view of a bosom.

I'm sure there were plenty of honest, decent folk among the company, and I resolved to seek them out. But then I was suddenly distracted by the sight of our old friend Eliphalet Brown, nodding smugly as the preacher enumerated the heavenly rewards in store for the chosen few. The vision of our old neighbour, sitting there proud as a stuffed boar's head at a Christmas dinner, proved too much of a temptation. So I slipped out of the church, knowing full well that the lecturer was good for at least three more hours' thundering.

In the street behind the church there lives an old

friend of mine, an actor's widow, who has no more fondness for these killjoys than I have. So I paid her a hasty visit. I knew she had a chest full of her husband's old gear from the playhouse, and I borrowed an old trumpet and a suit of stage armour.

Pausing only to slake my thirst with a bottle or two of indifferent canary, I hired a broken-down mule from a nearby stable, donned the armour, mounted my trusty steed, and trotted up the steps and through the open doors of the church, blowing on my horn and roaring out to the assembled multitude that this was a dress-rehearsal for the Last Trump, and that hypocrites should forthwith tumble down to Hell, along with those who preached piety out of one side of their mouths while they cheated, cozened, and gulled poor folk out of the other. Then I pointed my gauntleted finger at the gaping Eliphalet, and cried that he would be at the head of the hell-bound, then I blew a great rumbling trumpet blast square in his face. After which I turned my mount around, and followed the trail of his own droppings out of the church.

Whereupon that colony of stunned and sluggish black beetles turned into a swarm of hornets, and set upon me with a stinging fury. My steed was hardly a swift one, and these angry sectaries soon mobbed me. For however much they might fear my strength if we met in an alley at midnight, they were emboldened by each other's company, and vied to be first to strike down the infidel. Alas, for I could be an easy match for any ten of them, but they must have been a hundred, and each one bursting to display his zeal upon my poor broken body. Or perhaps it was just their eagerness to escape the third hour of that droning sermon that spurred them onwards. They hauled me down from the poor frightened mule, pulled off my armour, and began to belabour me with sticks and staves. Someone, I think it was old Eliphalet, produced a rope, and I thought to myself: you're for it now; they'll hang you up without ceremony.

But they make much of their so-called law-abidingness, and would not cheat the court of its due. So they trussed me up like a bale of hay and carried me off to the Court of Arches, where I was charged with blaspheming and riotous behaviour, and also with befouling a church — though I protested to the judges that it was the mule who should stand accused of this last, not me.

In spite of such eloquent pleading on my own behalf, I have been given my sentence: I must present myself tomorrow, clad in the white sheet of a penitent, and make public confession of my sins at Paul's Cross. Although I have cut many a purse in that crowd, I never thought to be at the centre of its attentions. They would have kept me overnight in some foul cage, to prevent my escaping, but I gave them all the money I carried (which was to have bought your capon) as a pledge that I would not bolt, and would come at the appointed time.

When I left the court, I found the angry mob outside even angrier. I think they were disappointed to see me walk out in one piece, when they hoped for some sergeant to appear with my head on a plate. They set upon me once again, but this time I was not encumbered by mule or armour. Still, they managed a few good blows and kicks before I struggled free and ran from them. They came panting after me — for they are a fat congregation — and I was only saved from further harm by the passage of a great procession.

Some rich Indies merchant was marrying off his daughter to a duke, and never had I seen so many musicians, jugglers, flower-carts, and richly-gowned celebrants accompanying one poor bride to the slaughter. But I saw my advantage, and leaped up on a passing cart, all heaped with blossoms, and burrowed down in this fragrant hiding-hole until I was ferried forth out of the neighbourhood.

The revellers, well-lubricated with good wine, noticed neither my arrival nor my departure. But this merciful escape route had, in fact, carried me even farther from home, and I thought it best to linger in dark corners, and make my way home late at night through lanes and alleyways, lest any of these zealots should be stalking me to wreak further revenge. I dared not come boldly to your door, lest I bring down a plague of Puritans upon this house.

You may chide me for my folly in baiting the sectaries so, for I confess it was a rash act. But it was worth it all to see the outraged face of old Eliphalet when the Last Trump bellowed square in his teeth.

"AND YET," I said to Moll, "he'll have the last laugh, for you can be sure he'll be there with all his holy

*Moll Cutpurse*

company to watch your penance tomorrow."

"I'm sure he will," she said ruefully, "and it may be good for his soul."

¶ OFFERED to accompany Moll to the Cross, but she said she had business of her own to attend to in the morning, penance and punishment notwithstanding. So I promised I would be there at the appointed hour, and she owned that my presence in the crowd would be a comfort to her. Still, she showed no apprehension, and took the whole thing as a comedy, laughing at the fools who thought such a sentence would curb her, and speculating on the contents of the sermon that would, inevitably, precede her penance.

I shut up my shop and made my way to St Paul's well in advance of the fatal hour, so I might easily secure a place at the front of the crowd, where I could catch my poor beloved's eye. But when I reached the Cross I found an enormous throng already gathered there, and I was hard-pressed to kick, shove and jostle my way to a suitable position.

There is always a good crowd for the Paul's Cross sermons: the Puritans, who thirst for lectures as a drunkard does for wine; the worldly-wise merchants who know this Cross for the Crown's own mouthpiece and come here to learn the Privy Council's intentions and policies. But, outnumbering these by far, are the curious masses who come to see their fellows do penance for the sins that everyone commits but few are caught at. Some days there is a whole company of penitents, a barefoot, sackcloth-clad chorus of those unhappy citizens who have displeased the Church. But today, with as fine an understanding of their audience as any playhouse manager, the wise clerics had decided that Moll should stand alone. And the crowd was larger than was ever gathered at the Cross before, in spite of the drizzling rain.

To one side, as if dreading the contamination of heathens, Eliphalet Brown and his brethren formed their own assembly. They stood like celebrants at a funeral, not partaking of the pies and drinks and salted herrings that the vendors carried to the rest of the crowd. They bought no ballad-sheets, disdained the talking parrot who would say his prayers for a penny, and even spurned the scarlet-coated monkey who begged so prettily for farthings with his little gilded cup.

"She's coming!"

The crowd fell silent. A procession emerged from the church: half-a-dozen young clerics, a black-gowned minister with a tall hat, and Moll, clad in a penitent's sheet of bleached and scratchy sackcloth, riding in a cart pulled by two stout sergeants of the court. Eliphalet and his crew bared their teeth in grins of sour satisfaction, or frowned in gloomy delight at the sight of the sinner. But the rest of the crowd sent up a great tumultuous roar of welcome, greeting Moll as if she were some conquering hero come home from the wars.

The minister, scowling his disapproval, held up his hands for silence, and said he hoped the few words he had to utter would be taken to heart by all his listeners, and not simply by the unhappy sinner who stood here under the scalding gaze of the public eye as well as under the eye of Heaven, which wept for her in her wrongdoing — and so forth, for a fidgeting hour that would sure have driven away the multitude if they were not so eagerly awaiting Moll's repentance as the climax of the spectacle.

But at last the churchman finished his harangue, and said, "Let the woman Frith come forth to make good her penance."

The two sergeants pulled round the cart so it would serve Moll for a makeshift lectern (for never would the ministers allow the bare feet of penitent sinners to descrate their own comfortably-appointed pulpit). The crowd pressed forward, whistling and cheering.

I was swept even closer to Moll, and could have reached out and tugged the hem of her robe. She caught sight of me, and nodded, and I could have sworn she tipped me a wink. But then I saw to my astonishment that her face was all bedaubed with tears and she was weeping mightily.

*Moll's Penance*   I AM summoned here to repent my sins. And woe is me, for I could keep you good people here today and far into tomorrow merely in the listing of them. Hearing the sermon of this wise and holy man reminded me of that which awaits us beyond the grave: a long sleep. The long, long sleep that ends only in the Judgment Day, when we shall all be shaken awake and asked to account for our sins. And woe is me, what shall poor Moll say to the Angel of the Lord, when I am confronted with the sins I have committed. For the Angel will open his great book, and peer at the pages inscribed with my name, and will say, "Make thyself comfortable, for the list is a long one."

But the Angel has come to me already. For I dreamed last night that one flew in my window, and said to me, "Moll, you are deep-eyed and well-pickled in sin, and for the good of your poor tattered soul I will take you on a journey this very night. In a twinkling of an eye I will transport you to the depths of Hell, where the weak and wicked groan in torment, and then in another twinkling I shall carry you up to Heaven, where you may observe the righteous enjoying their eternal rewards."

And, so saying, he bade me take up my cloak, for the road we must travel passes through the chill and sunless realms of Night. Then he made me shut my eyes, and lifted me on to his back, and carried me aloft like a great winged horse. We flew out of my chamber window and into the air. He ferried me high over the rooftops and chimneys of the city, higher even than yonder church-tower. We headed swiftly north-wards, so I thought — aha, so Hell is in Islington! But we speedily passed over it, travelling faster in an instant than a strong horse and a good rider could in a day. And still we pressed northward, and I said to myself — it must be as I suspected, and the Devil is a Yorkshireman. But the Angel, who could hear my privy thoughts as clear as if I'd spoken them, laughed and shook his head and carried me ever onwards. Then I asked him, as we travelled northwards over the Border, how could Hell be in Scotland? Firstly, his gracious Majesty was born there, and it would be treason to think his cradle neighboured anywhere but Heaven. And secondly, because it was perishing cold, and the fires of Hell would be welcomed in that country as a boon instead of a punishment. But still we pressed ever northwards, and I thought to myself — lo, we are coming into the land of dragons and sea-monsters. And just then we crossed over a mighty mountain range, whose sharp pinnacles glistened wickedly with ice.

Whereupon my angel did a headlong dive that made my heart stand still, and we went whistling downwards as if we were but a stone dropped from a high tower. Yet instead of crashing upon the earth, we passed into the ground, which opened as it rushed up to us and swallowed us up like a ravenous beast, whereupon we continued our journey underground. We passed through caves and corridors, across dank underground rivers, and vast gloomy lakes that had no sky to mirror, but only blackness. Finally we came to a sort of moat, with a drawbridge that dropped down at our approach with a great groaning of chains and a terrible clatter.

We passed through a series of gates, each one guarded by a pair of monsters. And finally we came to a city, and in the city found a great long street, like Cheapside, illuminated by a fiery glow from some underground furnace. The street was lined with taverns and eating-houses. We entered one such resort and found the place in an uproar — drunkards pounding their empty tankards on the tables, to summon forth a servant to replenish them, gluttons struggling vainly with blunt knives to cut into the joints of meat that smoked fragrantly before them. Next door was a trugging-place, where a great crowd of lechers waited to visit the whores, yet no matter how they shouted and knocked, the portals of Venus remained locked to them. Then we came to an open pleasure-ground where gamblers played with dice that had no marks upon them, and still rattled them hopefully and called out their bets. Nearby there stood a playhouse, all crammed with eager play-goers who stamped and clapped and hallooed impatiently for the comedy to begin. And yet the stage remained empty. The Angel told me the crowd had waited thus, and would continue to wait, through all eternity, to atone for the time they had squandered in sloth and idleness when they were alive.

Beyond the playhouse, in an open field, we heard shouts and curses, and saw several pairs of angry men duelling one with the other. Some fought with staves, some with swords and daggers, but all were scarlet as poppies, consumed with the fever-hot flames of their own wrath. They swung their cudgels and darted with their swords, and worked themselves into a terrible sweat, but no blow ever hit home.

Then we came to a great place of commerce, like our own noble Royal Exchange, wherein men skulked in corners, gazing spitefully at each other. One looked enviously at his neighbour's velvet coat, the neighbour glared covetously at the next man's fine Spanish boots, the boot-wearer snarled greedily at the fine gold chain that hung about his companion's neck. All around this square were many counting-houses, where misers crammed coins into their purses, which remained ever empty no matter how many pieces of gold were dropped within.

Hard by this square was a great concourse, where a crowd of vainglorious bravos promenaded up and down like peacocks, showing off their costly plumage and smirking smugly as if they possessed great secrets of state. But each one discovered, to his great disappointment, that he passed unnoticed among his fellows, who were far too busy making a bold show of their own imagined greatness to notice anything save the sad fact that their fellows' eyes were not upon them.

So this was Hell, with its full complement of sinners. Yet I saw no flames, no chains and racks and pincers, no leering demons tormenting naked victims.

The Angel asked me if I was disappointed. I said I was surprised to find that Hell was so like London. Heaven would be otherwise, he promised, and with a flash of golden light, wafted me upwards.

We passed through clouds that seemed to be made of swansdown and perfume, and entered a great tabernacle like St Paul's itself, but builded all of silvery light. We flew, miraculously, through a window of richest stained glass, wrought of gleaming sapphires and rubies, and landed in the midst of a great congregation.

My head spun, but then my dazzled eyes cleared and my dizziness wafted away like smoke, and I saw to my shock that we were in the midst of a sober Puritan congregation, a mirror-image of our own St Antling's, where hosts of sober-suited worthy men sat listening to one of their number holding forth in an interminable sermon. And it was, in truth, interminable, for the Angel told me that the lecture had no beginning, and would have no end, but sounded forth for all eternity.

I asked if this was, indeed, Heaven, and the Angel replied that there was naught that the elect loved so well as sermonising. Thus each man reaped in the

Afterlife what he had sown on earth.

"Each man?" I asked. And then it struck me that in all my journeying through Hell and Heaven I had seen no sign of womankind.

I asked the Angel where the women were, in the Afterlife, and my question gave him pause, as if I had enquired as to the whereabouts of the cats and dogs. He confessed that those ancient fathers of the Church, who had exercised their wisdom on the number of seraphim who could dance on a pin-head, had been equally vexed with the question of whether women, in fact, had souls. He was sure, for his own part, that virtuous ladies went to Heaven. He presumed that if they were not to be seen in the congregation, it was because they were at home in their celestial kitchens, boiling up the dinners in expectation of their lords' return from church at the end of eternity.

And where, I asked, were the less saintly sisters. For there had been no sign of women among the sinners in Hell. He had no answer to this, as if the question had never troubled him.

This ignorance, coming as it did from one who had set himself up as a fount of spiritual wisdom, made me furious. So I turned on him and roared that if there were no women in Hell it was because, in the main, their lives on earth were Hell enough whether they were saints or sinners. And I would take it on myself to seek out the women in whatever limbo of the Afterlife they were hidden in, so together we might set up our own Heaven, free from the interference of smug people and Puritans and men!

And thus ended my dreams and I found myself home safe in my own bed, and I am sorry for my sins, and thus does Moll Frith declare her repentance!

*Moll Cutpurse*   MOLL'S last words were drowned in a wild, high cheering, which came from all the women in the crowd. Only the Puritan matrons kept silent; they glanced nervously at their husbands and pursed their lips in disapproval, as if they hoped for no greater eternal reward than to serve up supper in Heaven.

Moll, her penance duly completed, descended from the cart that had served for her pulpit. As she passed me, I was all but knocked over by the reek of strong sherry-sack on her breath. This explained her maudlin weeping and her well-oiled tongue.

As she disappeared into the church, to exchange her penitent's sheet for her customary raiment, another outcry went up from the multitude — but this time it came from the bevy of Puritans who had come to witness Moll's comeuppance. So engrossed were they be the sermon, and what followed it, that they were taken unawares by the troop of small girls who moved stealthily through their ranks. Moll's prize pupils nipped no purses, as a mark of respect for their preceptor, but used their skilful fingers and their tiny blades in another undertaking. Thus, when Eliphalet Brown and his brethren turned to leave, a score of black cloths fluttered down to the ground like a flock of headless crows, where the little girls had deftly cut away the seats of their baggy breeches.

So the sober-sided hypocrites who had gathered to revel in Moll's humiliation were forced to rush away home in most undignified haste, with their own pious backsides winking whitely at the heavens.

*O*UR life, after these events, grew somewhat quieter, if life with Roaring Moll could ever be so described. In time, she grew weary of getting a dangerous living in the crowded streets and boozing-dens, and returned more to fortunetelling and the doubtful finding of stolen goods. When Mother Bunch died she left her alehouse to Moll, who said that she had no desire to make her living by other people's drunkenness, and besides, the old place had no life or soul to it without its late hostess presiding over the revels. So Moll quickly sold off her inheritance for a comfortable sum, which she increased twenty-fold by purchasing a share in a Virginia merchant ship. She said she sought not to profit unduly over her fellows' needs, but wished only to keep herself well-supplied with her precious tobacco-weed.

She became, in time, a kind of mother-magistrate to the underworld, who brought her their disputes and contentions much as litigious citizens take their quarrels to the courts. Moll had lived so long among them, and scaped flogging and hanging so often, that she was regarded as a kind of female Solomon, and her decisions were adhered to by all the thieves and ruffians who petitioned her. But she came to be as well-loved by our more orderly neighbours as she was among the tribe of foists and outlaws. Sometimes, on occasions of public festivity, she would declare it was time the housewives of the street had a holiday — and she'd pay the expenses out of her own pocket to make the Fleet Street conduit flow all day with wine.

So instead of coming to the tap with their washbuckets, they came with their tankards, and I never heard one of our neighbours complain that their scrubbing and laundering had to be put off until the morrow.

Moll, well-scarred by her skirmishes with Eliphalet, waged a perpetual war with the Puritans. There is, however, no truth to the rumour that she dressed up as a highwayman and shot and wounded General Fairfax on Hounslow Heath while robbing the coffers of the Parliamentary Army. Whether in fact she had a hand in planning this advanture I will not say, but there were some hungry Londoners of Moll's acquaintance who enjoyed their first good dinner at the General's unwitting expense.

She was sore vexed when, in spite of her efforts, these Puritans threw down the king and made a commonwealth. For she said that they were worse than a dozen kings, with their passion for interfering in humble people's lives — telling them how to live in their own families, herding them to sermons, and — worst crime of all — banning the playhouses, and driving the poets and actors to seek other, duller employment or die penniless. So unhappy was she at the way they ruled us that she, with some of our neighbours, led the great uprising of women against the government, crying out against their foolish policies, and the way they disturbed our peace and prosperity.

We were driven off the streets, of course, with the Parliament calling us monsters against nature, and bidding us return to our distaffs. But we made them tremble, and Moll, though she was ill with the dropsy that plagued her later years, made a fine figure, mounted on a white horse at the head of the crowd.

In spite of Moll's dropsy, which I maintained was caused by too much drink, we kept our health and strength far longer than the majority of women. We knew not whether we were strong because we had escaped the dangers of child-bed, or because we had been well-nourished and amply supplied with health-giving herbs and tonics.

But even with these advantages, Moll could not go on roaring forever, and the morning came when all my cries and caresses would not waken her. But I console myself by imagining her in some remote suburb of the Afterlife, cutting rich men's purses. Her body rests now in the church of St Bride's, near our house, and I know that very soon I will join her in the place that is reserved for me beside her own.

And there I have every hope that, for the first time in threescore years, I may lie in peace beside my darling Moll, without her stealing the covers off me as we sleep.

# HISTORICAL NOTE

MARY FRITH, the real Moll Cutpurse, was born in London in the 1580s. She was the daughter of a shoemaker, and was, from her earliest years, a tomboy, who would have nothing to do with the toys and pursuits deemed appropriate for little girls. By the time Moll reached her twenties she was a notorious character in the London underworld: the playwrights Middleton and Dekker made her the heroine of their comedy *The Roaring Girl*, which was performed at the Fortune Theatre and published in 1611.

Moll was, allegedly, a pickpocket (or at least a teacher of pickpockets), a thief, sometime fortune-teller, and — according to later legends — a highway robber. Even by the standards of her flamboyant era Moll was eccentric in her dress, wearing either men's clothing or a curious mix of male and female styles.

The law occasionally caught up with her: in 1612 she was sentenced to perform a public penance at St Paul's Cross for one of her many sins. According to contemporary accounts she fulfilled her sentence in a state of "mawdlin" drunkenness, having deliberately downed an enormous quantity of "sherris sack" to put herself in the mood.

Despite her vices, or perhaps because of them, Moll lived to a glorious old age. When she died in 1659 she was a relatively solid citizen, with her own house in Fleet Street. She was buried in St Bride's church, nearby.

A couple of years after Moll's death, an enterprising

hack published her supposed life story and final confessions: the work is more interesting as an example of the genre of "deathbed repentance" literature, than for any light it sheds on the real Moll. She is mentioned in various theatrical histories of the period, and appears briefly in Henry Fielding's comedy *Tom Thumb*.

Some of the episodes in this story are derived from these sources: the others may be as close — or closer — to the truth.